Rain

Barbara Winkes

ISBN: 978-1-0690835-4-8

For D.

Chapter One

Kelli

T he woman I love was forced to live a life based on lies and deception. That makes it even more urgent to tell her the truth right away. We haven't promised each other anything yet. We don't owe each other. It doesn't matter.

I plan to tell her about my second meeting today the moment I walk through the door. If it goes well. So far, I'm on track.

I haven't talked about it to anyone yet, not my former colleagues, my parents, or Merin. I thought I could go back to my job, forgive and forget, and move on. It turns out I wasn't able to. I couldn't go back to the team and work for a man who had all but blackmailed me to do his friends a favor.

I wasn't all innocent in it. I took the job, got it done, and decided it had to end there. This is why I'm interviewing for a position with Chief Brenner, to work for the local police department, where I'll be closer to my family.

I include Merin in that term. She's been staying at my parents' inn for a few weeks now. I offered to be a friend, and it's what I'll be as long as she needs me to. It will be easier on everyone if I don't have to commute to the city every day, have the same long days as before.

I'm ready for a change of pace. I'm trying not to disturb hers too much. She's still healing from the grief of having her life uprooted.

Brenner is still talking, and I wrench my attention away from my plans to the present.

"I see you worked on a few high-profile cases," he says. "I have to warn you, it's not like that around here. It's not for adrenaline seekers."

"Then it's perfect. I was never one," I admit.

"You liked the small-town living, then?"

I hated it. I hated that my former supervisor pulled strings to send me on an undercover mission far from home. The irony is on both of us because I found Merin—and I quit.

"I like the coast. I have family here, but most of all I think my experience can be an asset."

"I agree."

We both get up, and across the desk, he shakes my hand. "Welcome, Detective Jameson. I'll see you next Monday."

"Thank you."

If only everything was this easy. I take it all in on my way out, the station, much smaller than the one I worked in for eight years, the desk I'll be working at, and the window out to Main Street. From here, it's only a twenty-minute drive to the resort town by the sea where my parents own *The Sand Dollar Inn*. I've stayed with them as well, not ready to give up my apartment in the city until I knew for sure I'd start at the new job.

Next Monday. My commute will be shorter than before, despite the fact that I lived in the same city where my old job was located. I can't stay with my parents forever, and neither will Merin, even though Mom and Dad would never kick her out. We'll have to talk about the future.

As I drive home, trying to find a radio station that isn't playing Christmas music, I admit that I'm anxious about that conversation. No strings attached, that's what I repeated over and over. There was a time when we both were interested in more than friendship. She might still be. She also has to build a life from the ashes of her divorce, after fleeing her hometown. I swore I wouldn't make it harder on her.

What if she decides she wants to go, be on her own?

Merin came here to find me. She didn't have a lot of options, but the fact that she thought of this place first has to mean something.

At the inn, I see a few cars that weren't in the parking lot when I left early in the morning. I find my mother at the reception desk, frowning over books.

"Is everything all right?"

She looks up and smiles when she sees me. "It's been a day. You missed quite a bit."

"Are you okay? Is Merin?"

"Yes, yes, of course, we're all fine. Merin said to meet her upstairs for dinner later?"

I catch the speculation in her gaze. Not wanting to be lured into wishful thinking, I ask, "Lots of new guests?"

"A few beachgoers that rescued the young lady. We'll prepare a dinner for everyone tonight. Her boat washed up on the shore. Poor thing was barely conscious, but Merin didn't know a whole lot more."

Now I'm worried again.

"Merin?"

"She went for a walk with Sam, saw part of it. Someone asked her for a place where they could spend the evening, and she suggested the inn."

"Okay, this is curious. I'm going to talk to her."

"Kelli, you don't need to be a cop about this," Mom warns me. "She's fine, just wants to have dinner in private with you."

3

She looks me up and down in a critical fashion. "You might want to wear something nice."

I was planning to, but this is none of her business. "This isn't nice?"

"It's nice for work. You have a few more days before you go back, don't you?"

"Yes, until Monday. All right, I'm not going to keep you any longer, but let me know if you need help with that evening crowd."

Mom looks at me as if I said something silly.

"Go. I don't need to see either one of you here tonight. Take the time."

This is why I can't be living under their roof much longer. Time to find a place of my own. There's just one big question mark.

In my own room, I take a quick shower and proceed to examine my wardrobe. I got a few clothes from my apartment, but most of them are on the practical side. At first, I didn't expect my time here to be anything but a small escape before I went back to my usual routine. Read a book, take long walks on the beach with Sam, my parents' Golden Retriever, help out if I can.

That was before Merin arrived, nothing to her name but a suitcase, a new phone, and a credit card.

We have had almost every meal together since then. If I understood my mother's hints correctly, tonight will be about more than just dinner. We could have that conversation. We could...My face heats at the possibilities. Not likely. Not tonight. I try to find the nicest possible outfit anyway, a pair of black slacks and a blouse with a neckline that's the right compromise between plunging and decent. I'm flying blind. I have for the most part in this relationship, if you can call it that, because Merin is so unlike any woman I've ever met.

I don't want to make mistakes, not too many, not drive her away when there's still a chance. Is there? I sigh to myself and change the top. Some perfume.

Then I text her to let her know I'm home.

Dinner at your place? With an emoji, to keep it light-hearted, in case I misread the signs. Too late, I realize it's not the best reference to make to someone in her situation. To my relief, the answer comes right away.

Give me another twenty minutes or so, and I'll be ready.

I sit back down, catching my reflection in the mirror. Excited. Nervous. Getting ahead of myself. We're going to have dinner in her room, talk.

Maybe...I am about to freak out. *Thanks, Mom.* I don't even know why I'm this anxious. Wait, that's a lie. I know exactly why. We had to come to this crossroads one day, decide where we wanted to go from here, as friends, as something different. If it's the latter, something I started to dream about not long after I had met her, it will be a big step for both of us. For her, it will change everything. I'm scared to think I could be the wrong person for such a significant experience.

Perhaps tonight would be the time to discuss future living arrangements first—or the woman found on the beach. I have never been this out of my depth in a relationship. If that's what we can call it? She came here.

I wait eighteen minutes, then I go up to her room and knock on the door. I meet a couple of guests on their way down to the dining room, their voices excited and a tad loud. I did miss all that excitement, but I don't regret it. As I told my new supervisor, I'm ready for a different pace.

No more stalling.

Merin opens the door to me, and my breath catches in my throat. She's wearing a dress I haven't seen before, one that might have come from one of the local boutiques, and her hair in a loose bun. She's beautiful.

"Hi." The one word sounds a tad high. This isn't good. I'm supposed to be the experienced one. It's not like I've never seen her like this before, but other people were always around, people who made it hard to give in to the emotion. Like her now ex-husband. My parents. "You look gorgeous." Too soon, too much?

"Thank you. You too—and you're right on time."

My parents' inn doesn't have five-star suites, but the rooms are cozy and comfortable. Merin has set a table for two over at the window, in the little sitting area. With a battery-operated tea candle. Definitely a date. That doesn't mean...or does it? We still need to cover certain subjects.

"Please. Sit. I hope you don't mind I involved your mom in this, but my cooking options are a bit limited, and I wanted this to be...nice," she says after a pause, and I sense that wasn't her first choice of terms. Special. It's beyond special that she's even here, though I have to remind myself that her choices, too, were limited.

"It is. You're here."

Are we going to do this dance forever, like a couple of teenagers?

"I look forward to it," I continue, "and don't worry, I don't mind. My mom's cooking is pretty good. So is yours, but we'll figure it all out. I took a new job."

Merin's eyes widen, though she doesn't miss a beat as she takes the bottle of wine out of the mini-fridge and pours us a glass each.

"That's a surprise. I thought you'd like to go back?"

"To the job, yes, but I realized I couldn't work for my former boss any longer." I take a deep breath, and then a sip of wine. "It wouldn't work in the long run." I've been telling her that she shouldn't make too many compromises. It was time for me to practice what I'd been preaching. "No matter how you spin it, he was still chummy with the Gavins, even if doing them a favor wasn't the main reason why he sent me. The whole affair was...fishy."

I didn't expect her to giggle at that. Nerves.

"I'm sorry, I didn't mean to make fun of that. Come to think of it, nothing was funny about it...but I met you. I could never regret that."

Her frank statement thrills me.

"Same here. Now that we're both in the same place, I realized there was an opportunity. It's only twenty minutes from here, and it seems like no one will ask me to do them any favors. So far so good."

"I'm glad. I think it's time I find a job too. I can't exploit your parents' hospitality forever."

I reach out to place my hand over hers, encouraged when she doesn't pull back.

"You're not exploiting anything or anyone. Take the time to find out what you need. I'll cancel the lease for my apartment in the city, and I'll look for something around here."

"I thought you were wary of small towns?"

"I am. It depends on the people in those small towns. If you want...and remember, it's not an obligation..."

"You want me to move in with you?" The excitement in her tone is unmistakable. So are the residual doubts. I know she felt bad for coming here only after the tornado destroyed her home and her husband asked for a divorce to live his happily ever after with his long-time boyfriend. I know every step from here is a big decision, and I want to make it as easy on her as I can.

"If you want to."

"I'll find a job, I swear. And if there's a stove, I'll cook."

"You don't have to do any of that, but I think we can make it work. I...I've been thinking about you a lot. You have to know that I won't rush you into anything."

"I know that," Merin says, her utter conviction going a long way to calm my nerves. "I'm aware there's a lot we still have to figure out. I've felt more welcome here than I had in my own home in a long time. But at the heart of it all it's just me being selfish, because I want to be with you. Regardless of what the circumstances are. I don't know what it's going to be like, but I'm willing to take the chance. I can't ever go back."

She doesn't just mean a geographical location.

"You don't have to. You can choose."

"I already have. If you don't mind all the baggage that comes with that...me."

"You're willing to give this, us, a try, I'm the lucky one," I say. "Before my boss sent me to find Lucas Gavin, I had almost lost my job. I haven't been on a date in over a year if we don't count the time that I lured you to a gay bar. But I care about you. I want you to be comfortable." It's strange to spell these things out, with an odd ending to my speech. I hope that transparency will help us move forward.

Merin has never been with a woman. She stayed faithful to a man who still loves her as a friend, but never desired her. She told me they had sex once. Not that it's the most important thing—but it matters somewhat, doesn't it?

"Maybe what I need is more than comfort."

A few seconds tick by, and I wonder if this is the moment.

Merin jumps to her feet. "Instead of making insinuations, I should get dinner on the table. We have time, right?"

"All the time in the world," I say, hoping I don't sound too disappointed. This is still under my parents' roof. We might have to wait a little longer.

Chapter Two

Merin

What am I doing? At least part of the evening is going as planned. Kelli is here, dinner is on the table, and she asked me to move in with her. I should be calming down, finding my footing. Instead, my mind is overloaded with images, memories and sensations. The woman who washed up at the shore, the hectic activity I witnessed earlier. My frantic escape from the only home I knew until the Jamesons welcomed me here.

Kelli.

I want to be with her, so much, yet there's a nagging inner voice insisting that I don't have all that much to give to her. I don't have a job, and I only have a roof over my head because of her parents' kindness—or hers if I accept her offer. I wanted tonight to be the night, but now nerves are getting the better of me. Does it really matter so much? To me, to anyone?

She's right though. It might be strange to face her parents in the morning when we go to breakfast, like every morning...I'm in over my head. I've never felt this inept in all my adult life. It's not just my house, my former home, that collapsed.

At least dinner is a success, not that I had much to do with it. I set the table and heated the meal that comes with the room, in the microwave. Downstairs, the group that came to the inn will have the same. And again, I think of the woman, the confusion and terror in her gaze. I can relate.

Can I? None of those closest to me got injured in the tornado. I have my health, a roof over my head, and I have Kelli. I should be more grateful.

"We're going to have many more dinners," she says, sensing my shift in mood. "Many more opportunities. It's been an odd day."

That's an easy out she's giving me after my juvenile attempt at being flirty, but I have to take it. My mind isn't in the right place.

"I'm sorry," I blurt out. "I'm so sorry. This was supposed to be different."

"I know. I don't want you to put any more pressure on yourself. I just want to spend more time with you."

It's what I want, too. That, at least, I know. The air feels a bit clearer, calmer. The rain has abated too, down to a gentle tapping against the window.

"Thank you for being so patient. I swear I'll start making plans, soon." The images are intruding again, and this time, I'm not pushing them away. "I've been thinking about that woman, what happened to her. What she got away from."

"Mom told me about her," Kelli says. "I think the worst is behind her. The police are going to find her family."

She seems to sense that there is more to that story, for me. Rebirth. A second chance. This woman came out of nowhere, as if the sea released her. The storm drove me from my home. Thunder. Rain.

"I hope they're good people," I say, and instantly feel the need to correct myself. "Not that my family isn't. You know what I mean."

"I do." The small but noticeable hint of anger to Kelli's tone tells me she's not ready to do what I've been struggling with, forgiving them. They don't understand, how I could live with a man who's in love with another man, how I could fall for a woman. It's outside of their reality, and they want to keep it that way. For many years, I kept away everything that made me uncomfortable. The nights George didn't come home. The comments, "jokes", that were never funny or clever. A young woman paid the price for our collective uncomfortable silence, and it's a miracle that she never blamed any of us for her ordeal.

I'm still blaming myself.

"I think I need therapy." I laugh, and realize this isn't funny either, when all I want is cry, and never stop. Because I don't know if I will ever be free, or happy, enough to be in a relationship with the woman I want so much. I used to dress like someone ten years my senior, all the while I felt a lot more like the teenagers I was teaching. Immature. "Not for being gay, but for someone to teach me how to be an adult. I'm so sorry. I didn't mean to spend all night in my head and drag you to that sad place too." The house, the marriage, it was all a façade. The storm stripped it all away, and I'm not sure I can handle what's left.

"You are an adult. You've put everyone but you first for so many years. I'm no expert, but I don't think you're used to thinking about what *you* need, and it's about time. If it's a new job, a new apartment, or therapy...I'll support you the best I can."

"Why?" I ask the all-important question, holding her gaze, my heart pounding.

"Because I care about you. And I'm in love with you."

We might be going around in circles, but her words go a long way to reassure me. I wish I could see what she sees. At this moment, I have to have faith and believe her that this alternative version of me exists, the Merin who could get it together some-day.

"Enough to stay with me, even though tonight might not be...*the* night?" My face heats with a dizzying mix of emotions, anticipation, desire, and the embarrassment of sounding like I quoted a line from a cheesy movie.

"Of course. Though the dessert I know is in your fridge would help too."

Laughing, crying, it's all still close. She has a point.

Later that night, I can't ignore that something has changed. We've slept in the same bed before, close, in each other's embrace. For comfort. Kelli might have intended a soft, chaste kiss goodnight, but I cling to her, pull her closer. For once, I allow myself to feel every sensation, every curve of her body against mine. It would be so easy...or would it?

My heart is pounding again, for an entirely different reason. I have no comparison, no point of reference other than the warmth and bliss filling every corner of my mind.

"Goodnight," Kelli whispers against my neck, her arm going around my waist.

I'm stunned. Never before had I taken anyone seriously when they said they needed a cold shower—until now. On the bright side, perhaps I won't mess this up.

"I'm in love with you too."

Her arms tighten around me. Like that woman from the sea, I'm far away from home, but I'm safe. I hope she is too.

Chapter Three

Kelli

M erin is still asleep when I sneak out of bed to take a quick shower. She's barely stirring when I'm all dressed, so I lean in to kiss her temple.

"You can sleep a little longer. I'll just go and give Mom a hand with the breakfast. If all those people stayed over, it will be quite busy."

"I can help," she says, suppressing a yawn.

"Whenever you're ready."

Another kiss, and I leave. Most guests are still in their rooms. It's quiet as I walk down the hallway, pondering last night and the future. We came so close...and I was the one who backed away. I have to do better, trust her, her words and actions. Next time. Fortunately, I will have another opportunity. Soon.

On the stairs, I pass by a woman who walks slowly, looking around as if searching for something.

"Good morning. Can I help you?"

Startled, she turns to me, her wide-eyed gaze seeming like an exaggerated reaction. What's more, she looks familiar.

"I was looking for the breakfast room?"

Is there a hint of recognition in her gaze?

"Just follow me. It's where I'm going."

"Oh, good. I'm starving," she says with a hesitant laugh, her gaze still on me. She looks like...No, that can't be.

"You're staying for the holidays?" I ask.

"I don't know yet. I might have to if they don't find my family. The couple that runs this place is really nice. They said I could stay as long as I needed to." I'm proud of my parents though at times I wonder how they do make any money with the inn.

"They're my parents. I'm Kelli Jameson." They must have brought her to the hospital first. How did she end up here? "You are..."

I didn't miss her flinch.

"I wish I could tell you. I have no idea."

"I'm really sorry. You talked to the police I assume."

"Yes, and I'll have to talk to them some more. Yesterday I woke up on a boat in the ocean and I have no idea how I got there. I was lucky some tourists and a lifeguard were there to help." She keeps studying me with that intense gaze.

"Well, we've arrived," I say and point to the door with the sign that says *Breakfast*. "It sounds like you have quite an ordeal behind you. I'm glad you're okay. Enjoy your meal."

She takes a step toward the door then spins around. "I know that sounds really strange, but...You look familiar. Like we've met before. Would you mind sitting with me for a bit? Forget about it." It almost comes out in the same breath. "I can't believe I said that. I'll go in there now."

"No wait, that's fine. Let me just talk to my mother for a second, and I'll join you?"

"That would be too kind. Thank you so much."

"No problem."

Her story has occupied Merin. It has occupied everyone as it seems, and I can't help thinking I will hear about it at work too. I might as well get ahead of that. I step into the kitchen to say hello to my mother who gives me a knowing smile. Oh no, we're not going down that road.

"Hey. I wanted to know if you needed a hand. I was going to talk to the woman who was rescued yesterday...I didn't know she was staying here."

That sobers her up quickly.

"Yes, what a strange story. The lifeguard took her to the hospital, and she didn't know where to go from there, so we gave her a room for the time being, just until the police find her family."

"If there's one to find."

Mom doesn't comment on my cynical outlook of the world.

"She asked me to sit with her. When Merin comes down here, could you send her to join us?"

"Don't worry. She's not going to get the wrong idea."

"Thanks. I can get her some coffee and a plate."

"You do that. But if it gets too crowded, you could always take the dining room."

"I don't think that will be necessary but thank you."

I pick up a plate and the coffee pot and go join the mystery woman. I pour a cup for myself too. Her reactions, another small flinch, a hint of surprise, are those of someone exhibiting caution, making me wonder once more what, or who, she got away from. Not that being alone, out at sea on a stormy evening can't be traumatic by itself. I'm certain that there's more. She looks so familiar.

"This is all amazing," she says. "I hope that when they find who I am, they'll find a big bank account too. I don't know how to pay for any of it."

"You'll figure it out," I say. "First things first." She and Merin do have things in common. But Merin knows who she is. She has family right here, me, my parents. No matter how cold-hearted and closed-minded her own blood relatives are.

"You're not going to eat?"

"I'm waiting for someone. But we have time. If there's something you'd like to talk about..."

"I'm not so sure," she says between bites of crêpes and bacon. I wonder for how long she was in that boat, without shelter or food. "Everything I could say feels like a lie because I don't know what is true. Perhaps I'll start with something simple. This is the best food I've had in...as long as I can remember. I slept like a stone last night, which is odd. Shouldn't I have nightmares?"

"I think the body knows when we're safe. You're safe here."

"Your parents aren't easily fazed, are they? They don't know what happened, or how I got on that boat—or who might be after me."

"There's not a lot of crime around here," I repeat the words of my new boss. As I'm listening to her voice, taking in her mannerisms, the pieces start to fall into place. Even though that's impossible. Isn't it?

"You have no recollection of anything in your life before, your name, family?"

"I'm afraid not. And to make this even weirder, you're the first person that I seem to remember, even if that's impossible."

"Perhaps you've been in town before. We might have run into each other, and not realized..." Even as I speak, I know it's unlikely. When I come up here, I usually stay at the inn for a few days, but I don't socialize with guests much. I do pay attention to my surroundings, force of habit. She reminds me of a woman I once met...different hair color, longer hair. It could be her, come to think of it. What would she be doing here? Where was she?

"Maxine told me you were here." Merin almost startles me, as if I were about to do something wrong. That is ridiculous. Neither of us can ignore the incident that brought this woman here. Small towns don't function like that.

"Merin, my...girlfriend," I introduce her. My hesitation doesn't come from fear of homophobia—I think the woman across from us has enough of her own problems to pass judgment. I'm happy to see Merin is pleased with the term. "Merin, this is—"

"The mermaid lady," the other woman says, laughing. "That's what I heard someone call me, and as long as I don't know my real name, it's as good as any."

"I'm so glad you found a safe place," Merin says.

A few seconds tick by. She doesn't move, as if unsure whether to sit or not.

"Do you want to get something from the buffet?" I ask. "I'll get you a coffee too."

"You don't have to stay with me," Mermaid Lady says. "I'll be okay here waiting for the police to contact me. I might go for seconds though."

"Let us know if you need anything."

Merin and I retreat to another table from where hers is in our line of vision. Another angle, another perspective.

Is that really her? I have to make some calls, unobtrusively check with old sources. Minimal crime rate, not a lot of high-profile cases. I hope that's still true.

It would be a miracle if Annabel Roman was alive.

Wishful thinking, or an unexpected twist in a never solved case?

Five years ago, Annabel had gone to the police pleading for help. She needed protection from her ex-boyfriend, Dan Emmett, who was also her ex-boss, a greedy, cut-throat businessman who had kept the charming mask for long enough to lure her in. We never got enough evidence to justify surveillance.

Arrogant, with a mean streak, no accountability. I barely kept my cool around him when we met the first time. Earlier this year, he became a person of interest in another case, and somewhere along the line, my patience vanished into thin air.

Even though I didn't touch him, his lawyers twisted that last interaction I had with Emmett into something outrageous. My boss gave me two choices—one, a transfer to the middle of nowhere. If I wanted to keep my job, I could accept a special assignment and better not screw it up. Something that was also in the middle of nowhere, but only temporarily: Find a missing teen who had previously been charged with rape but acquitted.

I took the latter, found Merin, and found the courage to leave my old job.

Am I paranoid? Maybe later today, a doting husband or concerned parents will come to pick up the woman, and Merin and I can go back to the big picture, our lives, our plans.

"You're the one who's in her head today," Merin observes. An unspoken question hangs in the air.

"I'm sorry about that. Let me get more coffee."

I focus on the present moment, what I know is real. Merin. The future. My new job.

Breakfast.

"What are your plans for today?" I ask when I sit down again.

"I'm not sure. Walk Sam. Finish my book. I was thinking about calling George."

I sit up straighter in my chair, resisting the impulse to ask why. They were married. The quintessential high school sweethearts, except that their marriage was never more than a front, and it served one of them more than the other.

"I understand." At least I think I do.

She studies me as if gauging the truth of my statement. "I guess I'm curious. For so many years, we could talk about everything. At least I thought we could. Then the Gavins burned down our town, and the tornado did the rest. All of a sudden, it felt like we were strangers."

Every relationship she's had in her life, changed. I can't even imagine what that's like.

"It might be good to talk to him."

"I thought so," she says, relief in her tone.

"I wasn't going to be insecure about it," I say, making her laugh.

"You aren't insecure about anything."

"I wish. You have yet to know all of me."

"I look forward to it."

Merin blushes, probably becoming aware of all the possible implications of her words. She doesn't elaborate though, allowing all interpretations.

That's all I need.

⸺

Merin doesn't call George that day. It's brisk and cold, but sunny, and we bundle up and take a walk along the beach, all the way up to the old lighthouse. Looking at the horizon reminds me of the first time I came to her house, when we sat on the porch, with the view of endless fields and sky. *Do you miss it?* I'm scared to ask the question yet. Of course she misses home, the way things used to be, the way people used to be.

But a lot of it was built on a lie. I have lots of thoughts and opinions about a family that deserts one of their own for bigoted reasons. I keep them to myself, because I know voicing them would only make it harder on her. Because she hasn't stopped loving them.

"I know we talked about it a little, but you, changing jobs, that was quick."

We have almost come up to the lighthouse, wind tearing at our hair.

"Not so quick. It's been a long time coming. My 'special assignment' was just the last straw."

"Your boss, was he inappropriate?"

"Not in that way," I assure her. "He was...is chummy with certain people. I think he's looking into running for office. I just wanted accountability. I'm not interested in making the politics of it look good for him, and we clashed over that."

That's a vague description of recent events but going into details serves no one. It's over. Monday morning, I'll work out of a small police station in a sleepy resort town. Except a woman washed up on a shore, a woman with no memory, who looks like Annabel Roman. I'll talk to the lieutenant and make some inquiries. For my own peace of mind, and to make sure that history doesn't repeat itself.

"You don't compromise a lot," Merin remarks.

It sounds both appreciative and a bit jealous.

"I did it for years. Things have changed as they did for you. I guess there was a time when I thought what I could achieve was worth the sacrifice."

We have more in common than meets the eye. Merin and George were pillars of the community, well-liked. She worked as a history teacher, he was the football coach. Both of them put their lives on hold to support their students. They should be able to do that without the pretense, without having to be limited by bigotry in power.

It's not always that easy.

"I was very judgmental of you at some point. I'm sorry about that."

"We're not in that place anymore," she reminds me.

We aren't. Physically, or otherwise.

"You're right."

She takes my hand. I no longer have to ignore the surge of emotion. I'm happy.

The sky is starting to cloud over again in a dramatic way, and we take the path back to the inn. I realize that ahead of us is the mystery woman, perhaps taking a walk like we are. Every once in a while, she stops and stares out at the sea, as if daring it to give up its secrets, her story.

Merin recognizes her too.

"I hope she'll be okay. We have little to complain about, considering."

That might be right, but I'm also aware that she's not done grieving everything she lost. That doesn't mean we have to put our lives on hold once more.

The woman arrives before us. When we walk inside the building, there's no sign of her.

Dad is behind the reception desk.

"Hey. You two just made it before the rain. You're coming to dinner, right?"

I exchange a look with Merin, and she nods. I have yet to tell them about my change of workplace. Tonight might be a good opportunity.

"If you're not tired of us yet, yes, we'll be there."

"Are you kidding?" he asks, laughing. "You haven't stayed at *The Sand Dollar* this long in forever. We're happy to finally catch up. And Merin, you know you'll always be welcome here."

There must be something in my eye. I clear my throat.

"Maxine is upstairs. I'll close up here, and I'll be right up."

"Thanks, Dad. See you in a bit."

I catch Merin's absent-minded smile. "What?" I ask as we head upstairs.

"It feels like all I do is eat, read, and take a few walks. I have to be careful, or I'll get used to it."

"You've more than earned that time," I say. "But if you'd like to burn a few more calories, I have ideas for that." It's not what I meant to say, but it makes her giggle. I'm head over heels. "I mean, kids need history teachers everywhere. If that's what you choose to do, you'll find something eventually."

Mom is standing in the doorway of the private area of the inn, arms crossed over her chest.

"I think she understood what you meant to say. Come on in, have a glass of wine."

We definitely have to make plans regarding living space, I think as my face heats. Having your parents overhear the sexual innuendo you just made is too awkward at my age—or any age.

Dad arrives a few minutes later. When we sit down for dinner, I mention that I've taken a new job, closer to the inn than the city.

"That's great news, Kelli," he says, though not before the two of them exchange a surprised look. "So, we'll see more of you in the future."

"Oh, I think you've seen a lot of me lately, but yes, it crossed my mind."

"You'd like to move in here permanently?" Mom asks. "You know we have the space, and it's a much shorter commute than from your apartment. You're not going to keep that one, are you?"

"No. I thought Merin and I could find something halfway between work and here."

"Sure. You'd pay a lot less rent than in the city too—but you know you can stay as long as you want."

"Yes, thank you. We appreciate it."

"I was thinking," Mom continues. "You'll do things at your own pace, of course, but Merin, you taught history, right? I was wondering if you might be interested in local history."

Her eyes light up at that. "I found a few books in the library, about the inn, and the lighthouse."

"The only tour guide we had just left," Mom says with regret. "They were working out of the community library. You'll probably want to go back to teaching at some point, but if you'd like to have a bit of an income meanwhile, I could set you up with them. No pressure."

"That would be amazing!"

I watch Merin sit up straighter, the sparkle in her eyes. I cast a grateful look at my mother, ruefully aware of my own limitations. In rebuilding her life, Merin is going to need more than the prospect of romance—even though that prospect is sweet and promising. She'll be happy to have something to do while I'm at work. No matter how many times we've assured her that she'll have a roof over her head, having a steady income again will help too. It's a start. A great start.

"Great. Then I'll give you a few more things to read, and we can set up a meeting with their office. They'll be lucky to have you, even if it's just temporary."

"I'm the lucky one," Merin says, her eyes bright.

"You'll find a lot of legends. Some say there are mermaids around here." Inadvertently, Mom brings the subject back to the Annabel look-alike. Mermaid lady. I was so sure that Annabel was dead, that he killed her, and we were partly responsible for not intervening fast enough.

"We saw the woman earlier. Do you know if someone contacted her family already?"

"She told me she hasn't heard back from the police yet," Dad says. "What a harrowing story, to lose your entire life. I'm sorry," he adds. "That's not what I meant to say."

"That's all right." Merin understands who the apology was for. "It is curious."

There is no point in telling them about my vague hunch. I'll have to make some inquiries and go from there.

Come Monday, I'll be able to answer some questions. They can wait. Meanwhile, I can spend another night with Merin, dreaming about the possibilities.

Chapter Four

Merin

A nother day that has come with many mixed emotions. It's become the new normal for me. No more routine, no more denial, it's all right there beneath the surface. Kelli has been pensive, and I sense that it has to do with the woman without memory. I can relate. I can't stop thinking about her either, who she is, what—or who?—she ran away from.

I once thought of idyllic communities like this, like mine, as safe. Bad things happen in small communities too, to teenage girls, to grown women. Sometimes, to abusers.

But her story is not about us. We have enough to figure out as it is. I can't even begin to express how grateful I am for Maxine's offer. When I came here, I didn't imagine myself becoming a tour guide. I couldn't imagine anything beyond seeing Kelli and hoping she'd still look at me that way, with suggestion and desire rather than pity.

And she does. I enjoy every second of it, without guilt. But it's true that I need to work, earn a living. The insurance money won't last forever, and except for Kelli and her parents, every last person I thought would be there for me has distanced themselves. I know who I can count on. I want them to be able to count on me as well.

I stand in the bathroom, studying myself in the mirror. For a brief, difficult episode in my life, every piece of clothing I wore was borrowed, from my sister, from well-meaning neighbors. George and I found a store the next day that wasn't damaged and bought a few necessities.

In the past couple of weeks, I've been to town and spent a small part of the insurance money on new clothes, ones that fit my body and age better than anything I've worn in a long time. The old Merin would have never wasted money on...this. But she's gone, and nothing can ever bring her back. I don't even care when that elusive moment will arrive.

When I step out of the bathroom, Kelli looks up from the book she's been leafing through, her jaw dropping.

"Good or bad? Too much?"

I meant to be playful, sexy. But I'm still beyond nervous. She puts the book aside and gets up, comes to stand in front of me.

"It's perfect. I'm underdressed though."

I thought the white tank top and dark blue briefs were far from that. I hardly know where to look when she has so little clothes on her. Her hands come to rest on my waist, the touch light, inviting, not pressuring. I shiver. Words. I need to use words.

"You look beautiful."

"I'm glad you think so." She reaches out to brush a hand over my hair, leaning in. When her lips are on mine, uncertainty vanishes. I don't need us to have figured out everything, to wait forever. I have everything I need to know. Kelli takes a step backwards. I place a finger on her lips to pre-empt the question.

"Yes, I am ready. I don't think I can wait any longer."

Something changes, in the air, in her gaze, and all of a sudden the room is all heat and desire. I knew early on she was interested, and that I thought about her far more than a married woman should. But my marriage was a sham for a big part, and Kelli always saw past my defenses.

There's no need for any of it anymore. She's looking at me with unabashed, undisguised hunger, a hunger that finds its echo at my core.

We lie down next to each other, kissing, touching. Her hands are warm, teasing, and every contact is exactly what I need, deliberate, unhurried. I'm glad it's happening now, and not when we were still back in the chaos my hometown was even before the storm. I'm so grateful I want to cry, but I don't want to give her the wrong idea.

"I've been dreaming about you," she whispers against my neck. I shiver against her, greedy for sensation, eager to feel every single one of them.

"I hope the reality lives up to those dreams." My words come out in a heated, breathless rush. We didn't even turn off the lights. I don't care.

"It's so much better."

I can only agree. When she helps me take off the silky nightie that might not have been part of the essential wardrobe, I panic for a moment. What if it's nothing like she hoped? What if there's anything about me that defies the fantasy that we've held between us for so many weeks now?

"You heard me, right?" she asks calmly. "You're perfect, Merin." Funny how the voice I've internalized for most of my life always seemed to say, "You could do better, Merin."

We kiss again, a new unfamiliar tension building with every second. I might still be nervous, but I wouldn't want to stop, to go back. I can't. Her mouth is warm, on my breasts, my stomach...my thighs. Part of me feels like I should stop her, because this can't be real, not for me. It's going to be too intense, too much. Instead, I close my eyes and let her take the lead. I can't keep in the sounds, pitiful to my ears, but I can't bring myself to care. I've never before trusted any person completely.

So, this is what it's like. I have no regrets. I can't hold back the tears either.

⁂

"I'm okay. You must believe me. I've never been this okay in my life."

The gaze Kelli gives me is both affectionate and cautious. I can't blame her for the latter. I'm not embarrassed as I thought I might be. Instead, I feel...light, like never before.

"They're happy tears. I swear. I don't know how to say this without sounding really corny, or worse. To be honest, I don't even want to talk about it right now. So...thank you?"

She laughs, a warm, joyous sound that makes me all tingly inside.

"You are so welcome. You have no idea." She pulls me into her arms. My heartbeat is calmer even though the flash of a memory, a sensation can accelerate it again. I might be inexperienced, naïve, but it doesn't matter anymore. There is no rush.

There is no limit to what I'm allowed to experience, to feel, any longer. I kiss her deeply, tracing my fingers over her cheeks, her shoulders, to her breasts. Every action brings back the ravenous hunger, something that has been far out of the realm of my experience. It's not that important, I thought, overrated. And maybe, for other people it is, and that's fine too. I made choices back then, and I'm making different choices now.

I choose you.

Kelli might have come into my life for all the wrong reasons, but I know that this is right.

Kelli

I must admit that the tears alarmed me at first, but I can tell the difference. I never saw Merin this happy and playful in those whirlwind days when I first met her. I might take a bit of credit, lying awake late at night with what's likely a goofy grin on my face. She's warm, relaxed, calm in my arms.

I always knew it could be like this. I just didn't know if we'd ever get the chance. Most of the obstacles are out of the way. We'll both start new jobs, find a new place to live, where Merin can heal from the betrayal of those closest to her. Me? I might have to give up a few illusions I had about making a difference in the world. I'll live with that. The worst is past us. I'm in love. I know she is too. Time to let go of the past.

I have to get up earlier that morning. Merin insists on having breakfast with me anyway. Her smile makes me want to skip breakfast altogether, continue where we left off.

Routines are necessary. They will help us moving forward, and... "There's always tonight."

"I was hoping you'd say that. There is so much I want to try."

She did that on purpose. I don't mind. I couldn't be happier. "I can't wait."

The breakfast room is empty save for a couple and a single woman sitting by herself, no sign of Mermaid Lady. Mom comes over to our table with a couple of books and journals for Merin.

"This is to get you started. I can take you to the office this afternoon if you want."

"This afternoon. That's...soon," she says, uncertain.

"It's mostly a formality, so they can meet you. It's not like they'd find someone on such short notice. They prefer this to closing for the season, and you're more than qualified anyway."

"Thank you so much. I'll study these this morning then."

"Sure, but don't think of it as a test. They'll have all the material you need."

"You'll be great," I add.

"I don't know about great, but I'll do my best."

I have an answer for that, but I can't say it out loud with my mother standing right there.

❧

I spend the morning familiarizing myself with the cases on my desk. A stolen car, a B&E at a jewelry store. Those are the kind of low-violence, low-key crimes I expected. I read over the reports and jot down notes about whom to contact. It's quiet. I like quiet, tempted to fantasize...I don't. I want to stay here for as long as possible. The other detective isn't here now, but I talked to him briefly when I came in for the interview.

The officers I met seemed to have no problem with a new arrival in their small circle. I don't think any of them know Bill Cheney, my former boss, but they might have heard of him.

They'll understand I'm happy to be here. I'm almost done when I hear a commotion at the front desk and jump up to find out what's the matter.

Officer Manning is trying to console a crying woman. I'm startled to realize it's Mermaid Lady.

"No, don't touch me," she shrieks.

It's about time we talked for real.

"Ms...What can we help you with? You remember me, we met at *The Sand Dollar Inn*. I'm Kelli, the owners' daughter."

She quiets down, staring at me with wild eyes. I'm worried she might collapse, but then recognition sets in. I can see that she's still terrified.

"Why don't we go somewhere quiet and talk?" I ask in a low voice. To the officer I say, "It's okay. I know her." Sort of. "Let's sit and you tell me what we can help you with? I'll get you a coffee, something to eat if you want."

She whispers something I don't understand at first.

"Excuse me? I didn't hear you."

"I'll never be free. He won't let me."

I freeze, fighting the nightmare, the current threatening to pull me under.

"You're safe here. In this town, at the inn, and certainly here at the police station. I promise you that. Let's talk."

She lets herself be coaxed into the break room where she slumps onto a chair, deflated, the opposite of the woman I met the other day. She has jolted me into problem-solving mode, the fantasy of earlier far away.

"Are you hurt?" I ask.

She shakes her head.

"All right. Give me a second, and we'll clear this up."

I set a coffee from the vending machine in front of her and get one for myself too. I don't know if she had breakfast at the inn, but I buy a muffin and a small bag of chips just in case.

"I don't know how we can." She sounds utterly defeated. "Maybe it was a mistake to come here. I should leave."

"You're scared of someone."

Frustration replaces the fear in her gaze. "It must be that way, right? I have terrible nightmares, but I can't grasp one freaking memory. Just the fear, and...his voice. He's always yelling at me."

"We will figure this out," I assure her. I've given a lot of assurances lately, but I'm determined to see this through. She brings back memories of my own too. "Did anyone contact your family yet?"

An uncertain shrug is the answer. "I don't think there is anyone...except for him. He is everywhere. I'm scared he'll convince them to tell him where I am. That's why I came here, to say I've changed my mind. I don't want anyone to know."

It might be too late for that.

"Does the name Annabel mean anything to you?"

I see a flicker of recognition

"No...I don't know," she denies. "I don't remember my name."

"I didn't say it was your name. What about Dan Emmett?"

"How is this supposed to help?"

"I'm sorry. Could you wait here for a moment? I'll talk to my colleague and make a few calls, and I'll be right back with you?"

"I guess I have no choice."

"It's a good thing you came. Your safety matters before anything else."

I'm not sure she believes me, and that, too, is eerily familiar. I'll do better this time. I swear. At this point I'm almost certain that she is the woman who went missing five years ago, no body ever found. Where has she been? And is her case connected to the one that had led me to Emmett once again?

This time we might finally get him.

I confirm with Officer Manning that no family member has turned up yet. I warn her not to give any information to a Dan Emmett or anyone related to him, should they ask.

"That Dan Emmett?"

"Yes, him. I don't think he has her best interests at heart."

Emmett is married, has been for almost two decades. That didn't keep him from straying. Annabel Roman. Chloe Banks. He has a type.

Back at my desk, I make a phone call to my old workplace, hoping that Roger is available. I'm lucky.

"Hey, Kelli," he says. "Boss told us you're not coming back. What the hell happened?"

"I'm sorry, but I don't have time. Have you heard anything about Emmett lately? Anything worrisome?"

He pauses, the silence dragging on too long for me to be hopeful about the outcome of this call.

"You're calling me about this on your first day of the new job? Kelli, you know we supported you as long as we could. We couldn't tie him to anything."

"And you're okay with that?"

"I'm not okay with that," he returns, a hint of anger to his tone. "What is it you want?"

"You hear anything, you let me know right away. It's important."

"Be careful," he warns. "Last time, the boss only sent you halfway across the country. You want to keep your job, you have to let this go."

"And ignore that he'll keep preying on women? That's not the job I signed up for."

Frustrated, I hang up on him. Quick searches on Annabel Roman and Dan Emmett turn up nothing I didn't already know. What if she did escape? What would he do if he knew she was here?

All I know is that I need to find the truth. I can't find my own happily ever after if I can't find closure for these women.

Chapter Five

Merin

I spend the morning reading by the fireplace in the lobby, engrossed in the history of my new home. Given the proximity to the coast, those stories are full of pirates and legends of mermaids. Neither one exactly falls into my field of expertise, but I'm fascinated with them all the same.

Rapid footsteps make me look up, and I'm surprised to see the woman who can't remember her name, or her life. She's heading out, even though the sky is dark with rain clouds.

It's no wonder that Kelli is worried about her. She seems to attract danger.

Don't we all? I'm grateful that Kelli will be working in an environment less volatile than the big city. Then again, given what happened in my hometown...I don't want to think about this now. I get up to find Maxine and see if I can help her with anything.

She is folding a load of towels, smiling when I knock on the door.

"Merin. You're done already?"

"Almost. Those are fascinating reads. I hope I'll be able to do those stories justice."

"Kelli told me you taught teenagers. If you can hold their attention, you'll do fine with the tourists that come all the way here." She casts a look outside the window. "Come to think of it, what if we go right now? I'm sure they'll make time, and the weather will only get worse."

"Right now? I guess I can do that." The thought fills me with trepidation, but I know I can't hide from the world forever. There might even be a world out there more forgiving than the one I knew. For my former school, the fact that my ex-husband had come out as gay, and I'd been seen in town with the gorgeous woman from out of town, was enough to cast me out.

They didn't even care that I'd just lost my home in a natural disaster. For all I know, they might have thought George, or I, caused that disaster simply by existing.

No, it can't be that bad everywhere.

"Sally is a good friend of ours. She knows Kelli too," Maxine says, letting me know in a subtle way that being gay isn't a good enough sole reason to be fired from a job.

"Let's do it. I look forward to talking to her."

Maxine gives the pile of folded towels a critical look.

"Yes, let's go. These will most certainly still be here."

"I'll help you later," I offer. "It's only Kelli's first day. She might stay a bit longer."

Even saying her name makes me blush. To my relief, Maxine hasn't noticed.

As we take the road to the city, I can see the lighthouse in the distance. A museum these days, it will be part of the tour. I'm excited. For so many years I didn't think there was a life for me other than the job at home, my marriage. I've put off calling George, but after today, I might have something more interesting to tell him. I'm getting my life back together.

If only other members of my family could see and appreciate that.

Maxine senses my sudden shift in mood.

"One step at a time," she says. "Let's get you that job."

After a fifteen-minute drive, we park in front of the library, not far from the local police station. Inside the building, we enter the library, and a woman in her fifties gets up from behind her desk.

"Maxine, hello." She shakes my hand. "And you must be Merin. I hear you've taken a crash course in local history to help us out of a bind. I can't tell you how grateful I am. Come on, let's talk about this over a tea."

I almost cry again. People like Kelli, and her parents, make it look so easy to step in and help others, and do the right thing. At some point, I thought I was that kind of person, that my friends and family were too, but I might have been fooling myself. Caitlyn, who had been my friend since elementary school, up until the tornado and subsequent scandal, hasn't called or texted. A couple of updates from my sister Ellen sounded clinical. Fiona, my niece, is the only one who keeps me in her life. I can't change any of them, I know. It still hurts.

I know one thing though. I might be dependent on the kindness of strangers for a little while longer, but I won't take any of it for granted. I intend to pay it forward.

Like Maxine said, one step at a time.

Kelli

I can't believe what I'm seeing when I walk back into the break room: Annabel is gone. She took the coffee and food with her. I head back to the front desk where Officer Manning is on the phone and make frantic signs to her.

"One moment, please," she says and turns her attention to me.

"The woman who came in earlier, have you seen her?"

"I'm sorry, no. Is there a problem?"

"I don't know yet. Thanks."

Why did she leave, and where did she go? I can give myself the answer to the first question. If I'm as familiar to her as she is to me, if she remembers me a little, why would she trust that I can protect her? I failed the last time. It could get worse though if she's out there alone.

There is no warrant out on her as far as we know. I had no means to hold her. She was calmer after we talked, but I'm still worried.

I wait until Officer Manning has finished her call and ask her to pass the information on to the officers on patrol.

"She's not a danger to herself or anyone, but I'm afraid that she might be *in* danger. If anyone sees her, I want to know."

"Sure, no problem."

I wonder if she thinks I'm out of line, given that it's only my first day, but she's not giving me any indication. I go back to my desk, antsy, wondering where to look for the Annabel-lookalike. She can't have gotten that far?

The best I can do for her at the moment is to make sure Dan Emmett doesn't get anywhere near her. We need to know for sure. I sit down and call Annabel's brother Marc. I'd hate to give him false hopes, but this can't wait.

⁂

"Detective Jameson. I didn't expect to hear from you ever again." His tone is cautious, bordering on suspicious. Marc Roman has a point. I did what I could, but in the end, it was not enough for his sister.

"I understand. And I know this is extremely difficult for you, but something came up. I..." Getting ahead of myself? Does this qualify as a lie or as wishful thinking? "I have reason to believe that Annabel is alive."

"No, not that again!" This time it's undisguised anger. I see that the lieutenant has come up to my desk. This isn't good. I'm sure he heard Marc Roman yelling at me.

"Enough of this. Detective, I know you tried hard, but this is over. Annabel is gone. We, you couldn't hold him accountable."

"Mr. Roman, please hear me out. There's a woman here who was rescued from a ship in a storm. She can't remember her name or anything about her life before the incident. I believe we've found Annabel, and I need you to identify her. I'll send you a picture but seeing you might help jog her memory."

Silence. Seeing the impatience in my supervisor's gaze, I cover the mouthpiece with my hand, "I'll be right with you."

"In my office in five minutes." He shakes his head and walks away.

"Is this a joke?" Marc Roman asks. He's been grieving a long time, so I can forgive the offensive questions. I wouldn't joke about something that's been haunting me for many years.

What if it's not her, and I make him come here for nothing?

What if she disappeared for good?

No. All of us deserve a better outcome. "It's very likely that this woman is Annabel. She needs a familiar, safe person right now."

"I want to see that picture."

"Of course."

I send it and hold my breath. On the other end, Marc is silent for a few excruciating seconds.

"My God, that's Annabel." Finally, I can exhale, as he continues. "I'll get in the car right now. Give me an address? Can I talk to her?"

I wish I didn't have to curb his hopeful excitement.

"You have to understand she's scared right now. She ran, but I assure you that we'll find her."

"I'm sorry, Detective Jameson, but I've had quite enough of your assurances."

Resignation has replaced anger. I don't argue. I deserve every bit of it.

"Would you please come?"

"Can I meet you at the station?"

"Yes, definitely. If it's not me, someone will be here to talk to you. Thank you so much, Mr. Roman."

He doesn't comment, so I give him the address and end the call. A minute later I knock on the lieutenant's office.

"Come on in. Close the door, please."

"I think I owe you an explanation."

He gestures for me to sit.

"Yes, you do. How did we go from getting familiar with a few current cases to launching a search team for a woman who was perfectly within her rights to walk out of here, whenever she pleased?"

That's one way to look at it.

"Annabel Roman came here because she was scared. I know who she's scared of. I worked that case, and we could never hold him accountable. We need to find her before he does."

"She remembered her name—or did you turn up a relative?"

"No, not yet. I'm aware of how contrived all of this sounds, but she remembered me the first time she saw me. She came here to tell us not to give her information to anyone. It's all vague for her, but she knows there's still a threat. It's important that we find her. I talked to her brother earlier. He's on his way."

"And you're sure it's her?"

"It would be too big of a coincidence. I swear once she meets her brother, this will all be cleared up."

"Okay," he says, to my relief. "We'll see this through. Let's find her, have the brother identify her. All else will be in the hands of our colleagues."

"If she chooses to stay here..." Even as I say it, I'm aware that it might be unlikely.

"We'll see about that."

"Yes, sir. Thank you."

<hr>

I wait for Marc Roman and offer to drive him to the inn. He's polite, not overly friendly, but accepts my offer. He stares straight ahead, probably lost in thought. When the silence becomes too uncomfortable, I say, "We will find her. Every officer in the region is on alert. She walked out of the police station on foot."

"What if he got to her already?"

I shake my head. "No one even knew it was her. We were looking for relatives."

"But you got her photo out there. It was in the media?"

"Local. He doesn't have that much of a reach."

"You know damn well how much of a reach he has."

His words stay with me as we drive up to the inn. The rain has decreased visibility to the point traffic has come to a crawl, but finally we make it. We're both drenched in the seconds it takes to get from parking to the front door.

"I must be crazy," he muses. "Why would it be her? What would she be doing here?"

Dad opens the door to us.

"Come on in. I'll just need to check you in quickly, and then you can go up to your room. We serve dinner if you like."

"I'm not sure yet."

"Someone's going to call me the moment we find her," I say to Roman. I, too, have to get into dry clothes.

I hear voices in the next room, including Merin's. I'm about to let her know I'm home when she walks into the lobby, the elusive woman, Mermaid Lady, Annabel Roman by her side.

Annabel stops cold when she sees Marc, and he, too, freezes. Then she walks right into his embrace.

I can tell from Merin's expression that she is as startled as I am, if for a different reason.

"Okay, this is great. Let me just call off the search. Then we can all get dinner? I have some questions."

Chapter Six

There's no doubt any longer: The mystery woman is Annabel Roman, and she remembers her brother. She remembers it's safe to trust him. So far so good.

"Why didn't you call?" I ask my mother when I help her prepare dinner in the kitchen. The lieutenant told me we'd talk tomorrow, and not much more. There's still the matter of Annabel going missing five years ago, no sign of life until now. I wasn't mistaken. If I'm right about everything else, Dan Emmett will twist this to his advantage. And this guy never lets go.

"She left this morning and was back after Merin and I returned. It never occurred to me that the police were looking for her."

"I know. I'm sorry."

"Is she in trouble? Are you?"

It's all relative at the moment. "We'll have to piece together what happened from the moment she went missing, who might have had a hand in that. I don't believe she faked a crime. I think something happened to her."

"But she'll go home with her brother, right? Merin got the job today, by the way."

That's not subtle. I don't think she meant to be.

"Probably, yes, to your question. And that's great. Not that she'll have many tours in this weather, but it's a start."

"It is." I sense that she has more to say, but Merin enters the kitchen at that moment. We barely had the chance to say hello, so I use the moment to pull her close for a kiss. "Hey. I'm sorry I'm so late. It's been a day."

"I can tell. But it's all good now, right? You figured it out—and I found a paying job, thanks to your mom."

The message is the same I've gotten all day. Annabel's case will be out of my hands. I won't be able to turn back time, for anyone. We all must move forward. Move on. I'm lucky to be with the people who mean the most to me.

After five years, Annabel was able to reunite with her own family.

The clouds will finally lift.

Tomorrow I'll ask Annabel and Marc to come to the station for their statement, so I can write my final report. If they choose to go back to the city, where she went missing, another precinct will finish up.

Tonight, I get another reprieve. The rain is letting up some, still tapping against the window, moonlight sneaking through the clouds as we make love. Corny, perhaps, but that's what it feels like.

I might have somehow fooled myself that I had to guide her through this new phase of her life. The truth is Merin knows what to do, what she needs, and it turns out her kindness and gentle touch is exactly what's been missing from my life for so long. She might have a lot of time to make up for, but so do I. Her lips are hot on my skin, drawing me into a haze of desire, making everything else meaningless.

I thought I could help her find herself, as a friend, as a lover. But Merin had the courage to leave everything behind to be here with me. There was never a reason to be afraid.

Merin

I won't start until next week, so I can just lie back and enjoy the sight of Kelli getting ready for work. She's aware of my scrutiny, a smile playing over her lips as she pulls the top over her head. I kissed those lips last night. I kissed every square inch of her body, the memory creating a rush of desire for which we don't have time. Not now, anyway.

Maybe tonight. I'm not sure how it happened, but I went from judging people for putting this much importance on their sex lives to being...insatiable. I blame her. Who could look at her and not *want*...?

"Whatever your thoughts are, they must be pleasant," she teases.

"Oh, they are. It's a good thing the walls aren't thin."

"I didn't—" Realizing I was yanking her chain, Kelli laughs. "I deserved that. Will you have breakfast with me, or did you just want to watch me dress?"

"Hm, difficult choice. But I'm hungry." I get up from the bed and move into her personal space. "I wish you didn't have to go to work." My hunger isn't entirely for food. Deep breath. "I have some things to take care of as well, study a bit more on the pirates and mermaids."

"Yeah. You have fun with that."

"I could think of something that's more fun, but...sure." What happened to me? I give myself the answer. I'm happy, in love, for the first time in my life. That's no joke.

After Kelli has left for the station, I don't dive right back into my literature. Instead, I call George's number, which is still the same. A sleepy voice answers, and I realize that I didn't take time zones into consideration at all.

"I'm so sorry I woke you. It's Merin."

"Merin, hi, how are you?" He sounds a bit more awake now. Wary, too, or am I imagining things?

"I'm good. I...I went to see Kelli."

"I heard. I'm happy for you. So, you worked things out?"

I didn't expect the blood to rush to my face. I don't think *that* was what he was asking.

"We did. What about you? How are things, aside from the fact that I just woke you at the crack of dawn?"

"That's okay. I might actually make it to the gym before work." We both laugh. It's a bit awkward, but I believe he's longing for the same thing, the easy friendship we once had before we were forced to confront an uncomfortable reality. We've both moved on. There's no reason to be uncomfortable anymore.

"You found a job, that's great," I say.

"It is. When I left, I gave up the idea that I could be a coach again, but it worked out. We are both working, which is a good thing, because life is pretty expensive here."

So not everything is perfect. That's all right.

"You wouldn't believe it. Liam and I pay more rent for a tiny apartment than you and I used to for the mortgage. We don't care. We're happy here, we have friends, family. That's all that matters."

"It is. It's great to hear."

"Thanks. I'm glad you left as well. We made it out, Merin." Warm, kind, that's the way I remember him. During the last days of our marriage, I came close to resenting him. He had a plan, had it all figured out, when everything was chaos in my mind, the tornado, my niece's involvement in a rapist's death—Kelli, and my inability to face my feelings for her. We're past all that, aren't we?

"We sure did. I found a job too."

"Congratulations. You're teaching?"

"Not at this moment, no. It's a resort town by the coast. I'll be a tour guide." I make sure to put a bit more cheeriness in my tone, hoping it doesn't sound fake. It was kind of Maxine and Sally to provide this opportunity for me. I'm grateful. I want him to know that.

"I'm sure that's very interesting." George stifles a yawn, which, I know, has nothing to do with the subject and everything with the time of day.

"It is. You wouldn't believe the stories. There's an old lighthouse around here, and...I'm sorry. You don't want to hear all this."

"No, it's fine," he denies. "I'm glad you called. I've been thinking about it, but we were really busy here."

"Have you talked to anyone back home?"

"No. I think everyone said their piece at the time." I can't help noticing his tone hardened.

"We just let them go?"

"It's a choice *they* made, remember? We don't owe anything to people who stabbed us in the back. My life is here now. I don't mind talking to you. Those who practically ran us out of town, I refuse to waste any more energy on them."

He didn't always talk like that. We'd made a choice, a sacrifice. For nothing? I wonder.

"I should let you go."

"It was good talking to you." The familiar warmth is back in his voice. "Good luck with the job."

"You too. Bye."

I end the call, pick up my study material and go back to the breakfast room, where guests can get a coffee and a snack during the day. The sky has cleared with some clouds still streaked in with the blue, the sea laid out in a panoramic view. Mermaids. Pirates. A mystery woman in a shipwreck.

I get a coffee and sit at a table, but instead of working, I stare out the window. There's no reason for me to be restless—or jealous, not even when it seems that George is far ahead of me in everything. He always was. His relationship with Liam started years ago when we were still married. He fell in love. When we were lucky to survive the storm, he made a decision. He has family in San Francisco, and he probably had a job lined up soon after he arrived.

I ran away from home to be with Kelli, with no plan whatsoever.

"Mind if I join you?"

Maxine startles me out of my thoughts. She has a cup of coffee in her hand.

"Please."

"Everything all right?"

"Yes. I wanted to prepare some more for the first day."

"They might not start over until after the holidays," she reminds me.

"I know. I like to be prepared..." I look down at my notes and confess, "I talked to my ex-husband earlier."

Ex, it sounds strange. Husband, downright wrong.

"You don't have to talk about it, but if you'd like to...I'll listen," she offers.

"I'm not sure if there's anything to talk about, other than me being petty. He has a job, an apartment, and he's not looking back. It seemed like that other life, and the people in it, never existed."

Maxine puts milk in her coffee, weighing her words. "Kelli told me about the storm. We get some around here, but I've never seen that kind of damage up close, and neither had she. It must be traumatic to lose your home like that. You and your ex are dealing differently, and that's okay."

"I suppose he's doing it the right way. I can't imagine cutting people out of my life like that, but they did it to us first." My parents. My sister. I can feel my throat go tight.

"I can't even begin to imagine what that's like," Maxine admits. "I know Kelli will support you in whatever you decide. Give yourself time. Meanwhile, you have a family here."

"Thank you." Despite myself, I smile. "I guess the next time I call him, I should also remember he's on the other side of the country."

"Ouch," she says, and just like that, the atmosphere is a little lighter. This family is so good at that. I wonder how Kelli's day is going. Closure seems to be the theme.

Chapter Seven

Kelli

I have finished up with Marc and Annabel. I'm about to sit down for my report when the lieutenant calls me into his office again.

"I'll have the final report for you before noon," I say.

"Good. Faster would be better, so we can leave this behind us. Ms. Roman will go home with her brother?"

"Actually, they decided to stay in town for a few more days, then go home for the holidays."

I'll admit it's making me nervous to think of her back home, likely facing some media attention. How will Emmett react? He always claimed that the investigation into him was the failure of an overzealous police department. When I went to ask him about Chloe Banks, he and his lawyer all but laughed in my face.

Annabel still doesn't remember, and maybe she never will. That might be enough to save her. The next woman? It's not in my jurisdiction any longer. Out of my hands.

"Your former boss called me this morning. He says you made some inquiries into a former suspect in the case, Dan Emmett?"

"I asked a former colleague if there was any news after Ms. Roman came to the station. I wouldn't call that an inquiry."

"He was very adamant about me passing this on to you. As far as we're concerned, the case is closed. We reconnected Ms. Roman with family. If there's anything left regarding her disappearance, it will happen in their jurisdiction, their precinct."

His tone is polite, but the warning comes across clearly.

Day two. Wow.

"I'm aware."

"I hope you are, Detective. There are open cases on your desk, and I believe Detective Heller just came in. Once your report is done, you talk to him."

"Yes, sir."

I should have expected this. I'll have to keep my head down and hope for the best. A part of me can't help wondering about my former boss associating with the powerful and influential. I'm so grateful I'm out of there.

Merin

I exchange a few emails with Sally, reassured after my conversation with Maxine. I'll have a few tours with tourists who come before the holidays, one romantic escape, and some school classes at the beginning of next year.

It most definitely is a real job. Since the weather has cleared up, I decide to take a walk along my future route and have lunch in town. It looks like I'll be here for a while. The thought makes me smile. Plans. Goals.

A year ago, I had no idea how quickly it would all change. I'm going through a roller-coaster of emotions. As I take the path to the lighthouse, I think of George's words, and that he might be right. I won't stop loving my family. That doesn't mean they're right—or that I owe them anything. My family of choice is here. My future is here.

When the lighthouse was still in action, in the last years of its service, it was a woman who ran it, living by herself in the confined and lonely place. Most of the buildings in the vicinity of the inn didn't even exist.

In her time, a couple of sisters ran the inn. One of them married the town's mayor. The other one...I fantasize a gothic novel type romance with the lighthouse keeper. That will not make it into my presentation, but it's fascinating to think about. Two women, insisting on their independence. It could be possible.

Given the geographical setting, they must have run into one another.

"Hey. You're the new tour guide, aren't you?"

Here, like at home, news travels fast. It's familiar and somewhat comforting. The latter, because everyone seems to know that I'm staying with the Jamesons, and that I'm with Kelli. That's different from home: No one seems to mind or care.

I turn to the older man who spoke to me.

"Yes, that's me. I'm Merin Burke. Would you know if the lighthouse is open to visitors today?"

"It's not, but I can open it for you. I'm Eddie Burton."

I must have looked skeptical because he hurries to add, "It's perfectly safe. We light it up only for special occasions, but the former tour guide always brought her groups. It's a pretty view from up there."

"I can imagine. Okay. Thank you."

"You're welcome. If you decide to stay with us, I can get you a key of your own."

"That would be great."

He lets me inside. I'm grateful for my practical shoes as I climb up the narrow, circular staircase. He follows me, pointing out different functions, the door to the lighthouse keeper's quarters, and finally, the powerful light that was meant to keep sailors safe. We step out onto the balcony.

He didn't exaggerate. The view is breathtaking, and I'm used to pretty amazing views. If I get a key, perhaps I can come back with Kelli sometime. I'm already excited about sharing this with her. Excited about this little adventure of my own.

When we are back down, he gives me his phone number and the keys.

"Thank you so much," I say. "This has been amazing. I look forward to coming back."

"Did you know this place was haunted? In case you are planning on doing that ghost tour too."

"Haunted?" I laugh a little. "I read about the last lighthouse keeper. It sounded quite romantic."

"There are different stories going around, one of them is that she lost her mind. You'll probably find that in the library."

"Thanks. I'm going to do more research."

Isn't that what they always do, call a woman crazy, insane, when she doesn't fit into narrow expectations? A woman living alone, doing this job, would likely qualify. I don't know if that makes me feel better or worse. I tried so hard to convince Kelli that my hometown wasn't the only place where people harbored old-fashioned attitudes, that some would call bigoted. Perhaps humanity as a whole has never evolved enough.

If the lighthouse keeper is haunting anyone, they probably deserve it.

On my way to town, I pass a few houses nestled into the landscape, and, closer to the main street, shops and restaurants. Other hotels and resorts are more to the other side of the peninsula where the tides are lower and less intimidating. I walk into a few shops mentioned in my literature. A couple of them have been around for a hundred years and more, in the same family generation after generation. There's a rich culture of history and myth interwoven.

The joy that comes with these discoveries is an almost forgotten feeling. I used to love to teach, unravel the lessons of history with my students, until I started doubting that anyone ever learns from them.

One of my students was raped. The most powerful people in town turned against her and her family. At least she and the other girls are safe now, though no one escaped a painful look in the mirror. When George said we made it out, he meant many things, and all of them are true.

It's a day for reflection, without a doubt. I was opting for a meal, but when I walk past the café that advertises the best apple caramel waffles in the region, I can't resist. I'll do a lot more walking in the future. I'm having dessert for lunch.

I walk inside the brightly colored café where a friendly server indicates I may choose any seat I like. A table next to a window is still free, and I sit, slinging my purse over the back of the chair. It seems like all my senses have been awakened. Everything around me is more intense. I've been scared for so long, to go that far, to go beyond merely existing. I'm finally living. That's how I justify the decadent treat to myself when the server returns to take my order.

Only a few minutes later, I have the famous waffle, topped with baked apples in a caramel sauce, in front of me. Whipped cream for good measure.

"Enjoy," the woman says with a wink.

I do while I watch people on the sidewalk stroll by. Far away from home, but I certainly found many comforts here.

From my place, I see a black car pull up on the other side of the street, and a man in a dark suit emerges. He, and his vehicle, look out of place in this town, sparking my curiosity. For a few seconds, he just stands there and surveys the scene, a calculating smile on his face.

His gaze meets mine, and I don't look away fast enough. His smile widens. Embarrassed, I turn back to my lunch. I hope he didn't get the wrong idea.

He climbs back into the car, in the backseat, and the driver gets back on the road. Spooked, I take out my phone to call Kelli, then decide against it. She's working. She's had a difficult first day.

I can't freak out just because a man looked at me.

"Is everything okay?" the waitress, a woman in her early twenties, asks.

"Yes, thank you. It's perfect."

"Oh, I know," she says. "I tried this myself."

In the late afternoon, I walk into the inn to find I wasn't paranoid. The man I saw earlier is standing at the reception desk, and I know he's about to cause trouble. Kelli's dad is talking to him with a stern expression.

"I'm sorry, but unless you're a cop with a warrant, I can't give you information about any of our guests."

"Come on, you're not taking me for a fool, are you? I saw the story. Where else would she go? I just want to talk to my girlfriend. As you can imagine, I haven't seen her in a long time."

Oh no. I should have trusted my instincts, called Kelli. I reach for my cell phone when he turns to me.

"And here's the young lady who's not worried about her figure at all. I guess with your type, it's fine."

"Excuse me?" I go from worried to pissed in a heartbeat. "What's it to you?" I don't care that I could be wrong, and he might be just another guest. It's none of his business.

"Sir, I'll have to ask you to leave," Mr. Jameson says. "Now."

"I don't think you have to. How about this? How many vacancies do you have? I'll take all of the rooms, for the next couple of days. Once I've spoken to Annabel, I'll go home."

Not just another guest, then.

"I'm afraid you will have to find a room somewhere else. We're full." Sam, who has been lying on the rug behind Mr. Jameson, gets up. He gives a low growl, clearly aware of the tension.

Something changes in the man's expression, and for a few panicked seconds I'm scared he'll reach for a gun.

"Please, leave, or I'm calling the police."

"That won't be necessary," Kelli who has walked in, says coldly. "The police are here. I got this, Dad."

I've seen her like this before, when she confronted my niece's kidnapper. He had a gun.

"Merin, Dad, you can leave. I'll have a word with Mr. Emmett."

I stayed with her the last time. I don't want to leave her alone.

"Now," she snaps. Mr. Jameson and I leave the room, but we stay close by. Just in case.

Chapter Eight

Kelli

"Detective Jameson, this is a surprise. An unpleasant one at that."

"Is it? It seemed like you already knew that I'd be here. I got your warning."

He leans against the counter, every bit as arrogant as I remember him.

"You finally found Annabel, and I'm grateful for that. You know as well as I do that I'm not going to leave without her. She needs help. I can get her the best care."

"I can assure you, Annabel has all the help she needs. And one more thing: Stay away from her and stay away from this town. There are still people who are watching you, Mr. Emmett."

He seems to find that amusing. "You and who else, Detective? Your parents? The young lady I saw at the café earlier? Don't be ridiculous. I know you never liked me, and you tried to twist that into some case. I loved Annabel, and I'll do whatever I can to keep her safe. You won't stop me."

"This is a private business, Mr. Emmett. My father asked you to leave. If you don't, I'll arrest you."

"That won't be necessary. I'll leave, but don't get too comfortable. You'll see me again. I'll bring my lawyers next time."

I shake my head. "To do what? You can't force Annabel to come with you, and besides, she's already gone. Would you like me to see you out?"

"I'll find the way." He leans close, still wearing that smug smile. I don't give an inch. He walks out, and a moment later I hear the sound of the engine.

It's not much later when I realize I'm shaking. I'll have to take precautions. This was too close.

❦

My boss doesn't give me much hope when I call him.

"He asked about Ms. Roman, offered to rent a bunch of rooms, and left when he was asked to," he repeats the course of events I related to him. "We have nothing to go on, Jameson. If your former colleagues decide that the case is closed, and it looks that way, there's nothing we can do."

I know he's right, but it's frustrating, nonetheless.

"I know you care, but he hasn't committed a crime," he adds.

"That we could prove. He made a thinly veiled threat to my family. Annabel needs protection."

"You really think I have the budget and manpower to do that? She and her brother are going home soon. So is Mr. Emmett. He's baiting you, and you're falling for it."

That gives me pause. It's possible. Annabel turning up alive, but unable to tell the story gives him the perfect opportunity to pursue me, and what's worse, he knows which buttons to push.

"Be careful," the lieutenant advises. "I'll make sure everyone keeps an eye out. Did you talk to Detective Heller about the robberies?"

"Yes." I don't see the need to elaborate. Heller and I spoke briefly about the files.

"Good. I'll see you tomorrow."

"Yes, sir."

I find my parents in their living room, their expressions serious. I wish I could tell them anything helpful.

"I want you to be careful. If he ever comes back, call me right away. Better yet, call 911."

I can tell they have a lot of questions. I can't answer all of them tonight. I need to check on Merin. I don't doubt that the scene in the lobby has brought up some bad memories.

༜

"I can't believe he's here already. He's moving faster than I thought, but it does make sense. He sees Annabel as unfinished business."

Merin sits on the bed, looking pensive as she watches me pace the length of the room.

"He left, though."

"I don't think he left town. He's careful, but he knows that there's very little we can do, Merin." I halt and stand in front of her. "He abducted two women that we know of." Okay, that might be a stretch. We suspected him. I *knew*. We just couldn't prove it. "Women he at first dated, lured in, until they disappeared. Chloe Banks turned up dead a few weeks before my boss sent me to find Lucas Gavin. The case was never solved. Annabel vanished five years ago."

To my relief, Merin doesn't question my assessment of the situation.

"What makes him so untouchable?"

"Money. Connections. Lawyers that will always threaten to sue you right back, and of course supervisors don't like that."

Merin ponders that.

"I think I understand where you're coming from, and it's horrible if he did these things. But wouldn't he be a little more careful? He's a businessman. Isn't his reputation on the line too?"

I sit next to her with a sigh. "You'd think. He's using all of this to portray himself as a winner, against the department, against these women, against—"

I don't have to say it. Merin understands how personal this is.

"Then don't let him win. Don't give him any more power."

It sounds so good in theory. I hold her gaze.

"I'll make sure that you're safe," I promise. "You, my parents, Annabel."

"I know. We will be. It must have been tough, being forced to drop everything and basically do your boss's errand."

"Yeah. The thing was that he had a point. The police department in your town had a way of covering things up."

It's her turn to sigh. "I remember. Let's hope that this time we'll get some peace, and the asshole leaves town. What?" she says when I can't help laughing. "There's no one here to scold me for swearing. I don't think God would blame me for saying that either, about a guy who thinks he should comment on the eating habits of a woman he sees for the first time. I loved that waffle."

"No, you're right. No one should have an issue with that. Dan Emmett *is* an arrogant asshole. Come on. Let's see if my parents are up for an after-dinner drink. I need one, and I need to talk to them."

"Okay, let's go."

This is better than wearing a hole in the carpet. I'm aware that my new workplace doesn't have the budget to put multiple people under protection, based on my hunch. If Emmett doesn't leave town, I'll talk to the boss about getting reinforcements.

Until then...

"I'm afraid there's not a lot we can do at the moment, but I'll make sure that there's a patrol car nearby," I promise. "The inn is an iconic business in town, and it draws lots of tourists. Everyone has to be safe."

"I get that he has influence, but I believe he came for that young woman? Which is bad enough, but she and her brother are leaving at the beginning of the week," Mom says.

"Emmett is not a patient man and she's extremely vulnerable right now."

This is my dilemma—if he leaves, it means everyone around here will be safe, but Annabel won't be. I'll have to talk to Roger again, even considering that he could have been the one who ratted me out.

"What can you do?" Dad asks.

"I'll talk to a former colleague. They'll keep an eye on him." In an ideal world. I remember the workload. Meanwhile, my new supervisor expects me to consult with Heller on more local matters. Merin might be right, and one of Emmett's incentives is to rattle me. I almost lost one job because of him. "I just need all of you to be careful, pay attention. Especially as long as Annabel is still here."

"We will," Mom promises. "This will be over at some point—and we haven't even properly celebrated Merin's new job yet."

Emmett's appearance is more urgent than that, but it warms my heart that they believe Merin's new job is worthy a celebration even more than mine.

"True. Let's drink to that."

She fills our glasses again with the chocolate rum.

"Have you had time to think about where you want to live?" she asks.

I've seen a few vacant apartments in town, but of course neither of us had the time to even call for an appointment.

"I know that's probably unrealistic," Merin says. I haven't missed the longing in her tone. "Those houses you see on the way to the lighthouse, they are pretty. I guess they're out of my price range, not to mention, all occupied."

"Maybe not, but if no one has lived there in a while, they'll probably need some TLC. We could help though. We fixed the inn almost by ourselves."

"I remember," I say. "There I thought you were inviting me to spend a few lazy weeks on the beach, and instead I was fixing the roof."

Mom shrugs. "It was leaking, and you'd always been handy."

Everyone laughs. The temporary lighter atmosphere is a relief. I'm aware of Merin's speculative gaze on me and can't help wondering if she finds my handiness attractive. Busted. Amused and a tad self-conscious, she looks away. I'll come back to that later.

❧

Dan Emmett is not the first arrogant criminal to mock me, but he's the one who got away—and, apparently, keeps getting away. It's one thing to be cautious, to do my job. It's another to let him live rent-free in my head. I've decided it stops right here and now.

Merin gasps with unabashed pleasure when she finds herself on her back, my lips on her neck as my hands explore her body.

"This is a great finish to a strange day," she says, sounding breathless.

"Hm. I'm glad you think so."

I can hear the sea in the distance, and it's every bit the way I dreamed back then when every thought about her was taboo. No one can take this away from us now.

I realize I have her wrists pinned above her head and pull back slightly, loosen my grip.

"Is this okay?"

"Don't worry. I'd tell you if it wasn't." I can't find anything to dispute her statement.

Her face is flushed, her eyes wide, her body hot and pliant beneath mine. She takes my breath away. I lean in and kiss her deeply, losing myself in her.

I've never felt this safe, though I know it can't last. Not yet.

I don't see Annabel or Marc in the morning. When I arrive at the station, Heller isn't there yet, and I use the moment to call Roger.

"Before you say anything, it wasn't me who told the boss," he greets me. "If you must know, Emmett is gearing up for a media campaign regarding how the police department treated him unfairly. Boss is livid. How's your day going?"

"Emmett is already back? He showed up at my parents' inn last night, wanting them to give up Annabel's room number."

"That guy is cocky," Roger says with unveiled disgust.

"So, you'll keep an eye on him?"

"Kelli. You remember we have other cases here? Don't you?"

"I do. That doesn't mean he isn't still a threat."

"Okay, and here comes the boss. I'm sorry, I have to go. We'll do what we can on our side. I promise. Talk to you later."

I have no choice but to let this go for a while. Heller comes in five minutes later and suggests we go see a new witness in the robberies. The timing couldn't be better. I have already talked to Officer Manning about sending a car near the inn as long as Annabel Roman is still a guest. That's all I can do.

We drive out to the witness's home, one of those houses that Merin was talking about last night. It's painted dark blue, with white trims and shutters. I never really envisioned myself living in the middle of nowhere—the recent robberies being a case in point. I'm sure the wide-open spaces remind her of home, those parts that weren't marred by lies and bigotry. Could we make it happen?

A couple in their seventies lives here with their two dogs. The latter barely look up from where they lie by the front door.

Mr. and Mrs. Warren serve us a cup of tea while they describe the car that they saw leaving their neighbor's property, tires screeching.

"We know they are usually down in Florida for the winter, and they don't have kids, so that was unusual," Mrs. Warren says. "It wasn't until later that we learned they were robbed."

"Can you tell us anything else?" Heller asks while I unobtrusively look around. Rooms with a sea view. An antique-looking cabinet displaying an impressive collection of porcelain dishes. A different kind of traditional than Merin's old home, but traditional for sure.

"I can show you something," the husband says proudly. "I took a picture."

He hands us his cell phone. This is the good stuff. We can even make out the license plate.

"This is very helpful, Mr. Warren. Thank you so much."

He beams. "Anything we can do to help."

Bemused, I shake my head when we are back in the car. "Is it always this easy? Tea, evidence, case almost closed?"

"It doesn't always have to be complicated." Heller shrugs. "Even with the tourists, there's a limited amount of people here. Most of them going about their lives. I guess you heard there's not a lot of crime."

"Yeah, I've heard. I'm fine with that. So, we'll run the license plate and see what comes up."

"We'll do that, but let's get a coffee first. Can't stand the taste of the tea." He laughs when I look at him in confusion. "We got what we wanted, right? A little courtesy goes a long way. Let's go get that coffee."

"Sure."

I could get used to this, easily.

It gets even better: The car used in the robbery was stolen a couple of weeks ago—that's the other file I was studying up on. We find the car thief, we'll likely solve the robberies as well. For the first time in a long time, all the pieces of my life make sense again. I have to trust that my former colleagues will handle Emmett. Marc Roman will get his sister the help she needs.

And I will be looking for a place to live with Merin, because she said yes, all the way, to us, living together, being a couple. Life is good.

⁂

By the time I end my shift, we have a suspect in custody. He'll sleep off his drunken binge in the holding cell and meet with his lawyer the next day. In a celebratory mood, I call Merin and tell her I'm going to take her out in town. She's ready, waiting for me in the lobby when I arrive.

This, too, brings back memories of when she was getting ready to go out with me while I was waiting downstairs with the husband. The three of us knew then that change was inevitable, even if none of us could have predicted how drastic it would be.

"How about I drive you?" Dad asks. "You could take a cab later, in case you'd like a glass."

"That would be great. Thank you. I'll just go change, and we can go."

Seeing how Merin is dressed, I know two things. It would be too cold to go on foot, and I am woefully underdressed next to her. "I'll hurry."

It's funny, in a way, given the situation that we're in, to have my father drive us to a date. Merin is not the only one who's been feeling like a teenager lately.

When we sit at a cloth-covered table in the best restaurant in town, I ask her, "You've been thinking about those houses some more? I went to one of them today."

"Really? I was just, I don't know, making conversation."

"It looked pretty nice. A bit remote, but it wouldn't be too far from your tours. And far enough from the beach so there's no flooding."

"There's just one problem," she reminds me. "There were people living in that house, right?"

"That one, yes. But we could look around and find something similar. Make it our own."

I had a roommate in college and lived on my own after that. Merin had a husband who was basically her roommate. This will be new and exciting, and a bit scary, for both of us.

She takes a sip of her wine. "That would be nice, but it doesn't have to be right away. We could also think of something else. If we find an apartment closer to town, we both could walk to work."

Either way, I'm saying goodbye to the city for a long time to come—perhaps for good even. I find that the thought doesn't scare me as much as it might have had a year ago.

"Let's look at a few places soon. That will help us make a decision."

A car passes down the road, and I sit up straight.

"What is it?" Merin asks, alarmed.

"Nothing," I say as the taillights disappear in the distance. "I thought I saw Emmett's car, but Roger told me this morning he's already back in the city, and on a media spree. I don't think it could have been him."

The waiter brings our dishes, and I force myself to focus on the delicious food on my plate. We're supposed to celebrate, move forward. That's what we'll do.

"You know, if we lived in one of those little houses, we wouldn't have to worry about...thin walls," Merin remarks.

She knows how to focus my attention.

"You keep coming back to that."

"Right? Look what you did. I can't get enough."

"Anything you need," I say, the words coming rushing out in a lusty tone. I reach for my water. This is only the second course. I, we, need to learn to pace ourselves.

Chapter Nine

Merin

K elli has lined up a couple of places for us to visit after work. After a few care-free and relaxed days without incidents, she's back to being stressed and tense. I realize it's because today is my first day at work. I'll start at the office, do one tour from there, and another one in the afternoon. Then I'll meet with Sally to discuss how it went.

I can't wait.

The lighthouse museum will be open all day, so I'll be able to take both groups there. We'll swing by the inn with the morning group to have lunch.

"It will be fine. You said it yourself, Annabel and Marc are about to leave, and even if Emmett was still in town, he'd have no reason to stay any longer. He has a business to run. Your former department will take care of the rest," I sum up the situation.

Kelli looks self-conscious.

"Am I that predictable?"

"A little," I admit. "You go do the job you have here, I'll do mine. Did I tell you I strongly suspect the woman who ran *The Sand Dollar Inn* fifty-something years ago was the lighthouse keeper's lesbian lover?"

"Really? That's interesting. Is it part of your tour?"

"No." I'm glad I managed to make her relax some. I could always think of other ways—insatiable—but there's no time for this now. "Let's go. I don't want to be late on the first day."

⁂

I loved my hometown, the scenery, the familiarity of the landscape. We took the good with the bad, the storms, the destruction, the gratitude when our town was spared.

As I look back, this seems utterly selfish to me. Many people that day were grateful that it wasn't their family, that their homes weren't impacted.

But mine was gone, including everything material that ever mattered to me, with one exception.

Today, the first day of my job, I'm wearing the bracelet Kelli gave me for my last birthday. It seemed improper at the time, to give a piece of beautiful jewelry to a married woman. I'm beyond happy to have it.

I love this town too, not just because the people in it have welcomed me. There's something familiar about it, living with nature, having to learn to respect the elements, or living with the consequences if you don't. You can't get away from it. It makes many of our other problems seem small in comparison.

Sally greets me with a smile and a firm handshake.

"I'd ask if you're ready, but you're early and you're radiating happiness, so I think that's not necessary."

"I am. Again, thank you so much for giving me this chance."

"You arrived at the right time," she says. "I have close to a dozen people waiting for you to show them around. Enjoy, and make sure they come back." With a laugh, she adds, "No pressure."

"Got it."

I follow her through a door in the back to the area where my first group is assembled. She steps back and lets me take the lead.

"Hi, thank you for coming. I'm Merin Burke, and I'll be your tour guide this morning."

...your history teacher.

"We'll visit the lighthouse museum and a few other locations along the way. I'll show you where pirates were active. At noon, we'll finish at *The Sand Dollar Inn* for a lunch break. Do you have any questions?"

I look at their eager faces, families with children, two couples, a single woman. The teenager with one of the families looks bored, but two younger children, a boy and a girl, look excited.

"Were there any mermaids?" he asks.

"According to the legends, yes. I'll show you later where sailors claimed they saw one. To the entire group, I say. "Shall we start?"

When no one objects, I take a deep breath. So far so good. I can do this.

❦

As expected, the lighthouse is the highlight of the tour. I wait downstairs with the single woman who says she has a fear of heights, one of the couples who don't give an explanation, and the dad who has stayed with the child that's too young to go up. So far, everyone seems to be content with what I have to offer.

The little boy was ecstatic about the place of the mermaid sighting. I can't help thinking that back home, this might have caused a derisive comment, as would the sparkly nail polish he's wearing.

Here, no one said anything, his enthusiasm infectious to all of us. The weather has held for the past few days, cool and windy, but sunny, the majestic nature a perfect backdrop to my mix of local history and storytelling.

I touch on the story of the woman lighthouse keeper, Louisa Bennett, but keep my theories about her to myself.

"Must have been lonely up there, all by herself," the single woman says when everyone is back on the ground. "Did you know if she had any companion?"

"I found no source for that," I admit. "Maybe she enjoyed being by herself."

"Or she was punished for something," one of the husbands jokes, his wife slapping his arm.

"I'm afraid there's nothing to support that idea either but given the fact that she kept that job for nearly a decade, we can imagine she was an independent woman." Who, occasionally, visited the innkeeper, and they likely had a passionate love affair. As friendly as everyone has been, I don't think Sally would appreciate me going off script like this on the first day.

"There's a porcelain ware store I'd like to show you that's been around for many generations. After that, we'll head to the inn for lunch?"

Everyone agrees. This was almost too easy, but I'm not going to question a good thing.

At the inn I introduce the group to Maxine, and we sit down for a light but delicious lunch. I talk to the mother of the mermaid fan who tells me he's been obsessed with the mythical creatures for a while.

"He was so excited when we told him we'd come here," she says, shaking her head. "You made his day."

"I'm happy to hear that."

I needed this, so much, beyond the safe space Kelli and her parents gave me. Beyond the intensity of my feelings for her, both healing and frightening.

I'm back out in the real world, and I quite like it.

The second group is a bit smaller, but more of a challenge. I barely keep the older kids from wandering off on various occasions. One of the couples mostly occupied with themselves. It's a good thing I had a different experience first, so Sally won't lose faith in me, and neither will I.

The sky is clouding over again, and towards the end of the tour it starts raining. I keep my smile and cheery tone, but I can't help fantasizing about being back home, maybe have a drink with Kelli by the fireplace in the lobby later.

My fantasy must end there. I'm still on the clock.

Sally is blissfully unperturbed by my mixed experiences.

"You didn't lose anyone?"

"No."

"No one fell off the lighthouse?"

"Not that I'm aware, no. Just the view wasn't as great for the second group, with the clouds moving in."

"Then they'll live. The ones that enjoyed it will talk about it, and that's all we need. You did great, Merin."

I feel so needy, but it's amazing to hear that. Still. Moments like this are a sober reality check—no matter how much progress I've made, I'm still grieving over the sudden loss of everything I might have taken for granted, the support of my family and community, my marriage, and my home. I'm going to make a new home with Kelli.

Perhaps, one day...but it's much too early to think about.

Sally and I both jump when we hear the siren of a police car nearby. And then another one.

"A car accident, maybe. Do you want to go home or wait a little? Maybe Kelli's off the clock too."

"I think I'll drive," I say. "Whatever that was, maybe they need her too." My heart is hammering all of a sudden even though the sound is distant now. So far, I have with success suppressed the thought that Kelli's job can come with difficult traumatic sights, even here in a small town. I pray it's nothing too bad. Nevertheless, I know she's on edge because of Emmett, and I want to comfort her best I can.

"Thank you for everything, Sally. I'll see you tomorrow."

"Thank you, Merin. Have a good evening."

When I drive back to the inn, another police car passes me by. The station doesn't have that many officers. I'm tense and worried, even more so when I arrive at a checkpoint, close to the porcelain shop we visited earlier on the tour.

"I'm going to *The Sand Dollar Inn*. My name is Merin Burke, I live there." I want to ask him what happened, but I don't dare. Instead, I wait until he waves me through and continue on my way, driving as fast as I can without attracting the attention of the police. It looks like theirs is focused elsewhere.

I can't see any accident on my way. After parking in the usual spot, I head to the front door and let myself in. Kelli isn't here yet. The reception desk is dark, and so I all but jog up to her parents' quarters.

Mr. Jameson opens the door to me, looking serious. I realize I came close to pounding on the door.

"Merin. What's the matter?"

"Is Kelli okay?"

"Yes. She said to let you know she'll be home late today."

I sink against the doorframe, feeling overly dramatic. "I didn't mean to disturb you, but I heard the sirens earlier. Do you know if there was an accident nearby?"

I can tell from the alarm on his face that I won't like the answer.

"Didn't you hear? Ms. Roman's brother was stabbed. They don't know if he'll make it."

Naïve little Merin who always expects the best outcome, always looking for the best in people.

Dan Emmett didn't go home. Marc Roman was the last person to stand between him and his goal, get to Annabel.

What other explanation is there?

Chapter Ten

Kelli

It's Annabel Roman on the phone, and all hell breaks loose.

"I need you to come here right now! Help me! He killed him!"

"Annabel, what happened? Where are you?"

With a tearful voice she describes a building that houses a gift shop and an ice cream parlor.

"He stabbed Marc, and then he ran. In broad daylight!"

Arrogant. Cocky.

I'm on autopilot for the next steps, sending officers in the area to her location, and an ambulance as well. I keep her on the phone with me, gesturing for Heller to follow me.

"I'm on my way, Annabel, okay? An ambulance will be with you in a short time. I'll meet you at the hospital."

"I'm scared it's too late," she cries. "I can't feel a pulse."

Damn it. Damn *him*. Marc Roman waited five years to see his sister again, only to be murdered by the man who took her? This can't happen.

Heller follows right along. I can tell from the barely hidden shock that violent crime like this is something they don't deal with here, at least not often. I have no words to console him. I knew this wasn't over.

When we arrive at the scene, the ambulance has left already.

Officer Manning comes running over to us. "I've had one of the officers go to the hospital with them. It doesn't look good."

I suppress the urge to curse, only because it wouldn't do any good, for Annabel, for Marc. "Was she able to make a statement?"

"In shock, but she said a man dressed in black, with sunglasses and a baseball cap, came up to them and stabbed her brother."

"No other witnesses?" I ask in disbelief.

"Just a young mom and her toddler, she saw him running behind those houses. She ran into the store with the kid and called 911. The owner of the shop was in the back, didn't see anything."

I glance in the direction she pointed out.

"Did he have a car, anyone waiting for him?"

Manning lifts her shoulders in a defeated shrug.

"We haven't figured that out yet. Roman was too busy tending to her brother. No one heard a car."

"Could be random," Heller muses. "Tourists do get mugged sometimes."

"Not like this." I shake my head. "This wasn't random, and Emmett wouldn't risk getting his hands dirty in plain sight. He paid someone. I want to know where Emmett is staying."

He gives me an incredulous look. "We have no proof whatsoever."

"We'll find it. We have to. He came here for Annabel, not counting in that we had already contacted her brother. We have to bring him in, check his alibi."

"I'd like to check with the boss first," Heller says, still doubtful. "You have history with that Emmett guy. Perhaps you should take a step back."

"How many attempted murders have you investigated?"

"That's not the point." He's not offended. "We'll get help from the county. You should be careful."

If one more person tells me that, I'm going to explode. Count to ten. Deep breath.

"Once we're done here, let's go see Annabel. Maybe she can add something that helps us."

I'm not looking forward to that conversation. Most of all I'm scared of the obvious—that she'll think I let her down. Again.

I was right. Emmett never left town, all those interviews he was about to give nothing but a diversion.

Marc Roman might pay with his life for our lack of attention.

Heller drives on the way to the hospital, and I use the time to call my parents and ask them to let Merin know I'll be home late.

"You know this guy well," he states after I end the call.

"A lot better than I care to. I'm telling you, he's taunting us." First with words, then with violence. Emmett's usual M.O.

"Then it's even more important that we do this by the book..."

"Don't worry, that's exactly what I intend to do."

Annabel sits in the waiting room slumped over, crying. An officer stays at a respectful distance. I'm so glad they finally got the message. I was never exaggerating when I told them this man was dangerous. I sit down next to her and take her hand.

"Annabel, I'm so sorry. How is he?"

She stares at me with bleak, tear-filled eyes. "They haven't said anything yet. I can't lose him! I was just starting to feel like a normal person, with a life, a story...I was remembering things we did as children, everyday scenes with our parents. He's a good man."

"I know. He never gave up hope."

"It is all my fault!"

There's something she and I have in common, an eagerness to accept blame. It's easier to see through the misconception when it's someone else.

"No, that's not true. Marc knew that Dan was dangerous. He wanted to protect you."

"You really think Dan sent him?" She groans in frustration. "I want to remember more, and I'm scared whenever I do. Five years. Nothing about that can be good, right? I want to be oblivious, but it makes me feel like I failed. That other woman, the police, and now Marc."

"You didn't fail anyone. You survived. And we'll make sure it stays that way."

"Are you going to arrest Dan?"

Heller shoots me a warning look.

"We'll have to tie him to the man who stabbed Marc. There's a limited amount of people here," I throw a version of Heller's words back at him. "We'll find him."

"I don't know. I just want all of this to end."

Me too, I think.

We both get to our feet when the surgeon comes in. I hold my breath, maybe even send a prayer. Whatever helps.

Chapter Eleven

Merin

I feel a bit better after Kelli sends me a text. She'll still be tied up at work, but it's nothing dangerous for the moment, at least not for her. Marc Roman is still in the hospital, and he and Annabel are guarded by a uniformed officer.

Her supervisor and her colleagues have understood that Dan Emmett is a dangerous man with a wide reach.

It will be a while until she comes home. There's no need to worry. Is there?

Maxine comes to knock on my door. I can tell that the events of the day are on her mind too.

"Would you like to have dinner with us?" she asks. "I'm sure Kelli will be home really late."

"If that's okay, yes, thank you."

"Of course."

Over dinner, Kelli's parents talk about the upcoming holidays, to distract me or them, I'm not sure. Christmas, like Thanksgiving, used to be a big deal for me. With a start, I realize that this year would have been George's and my turn to host the entire family. If there was still a house, a marriage. A family.

I'm no longer hungry. I haven't forgotten my pledge to support Kelli in what she's going through. My own demons linger.

"There's been snow in the forecast," Maxine says. "We don't always get a lot here, but we still have to watch out. The roads can be tricky."

"I'll have a few more groups next week, but we'll stop over the holidays," I say. "Then it's going to be the school classes."

"Did you have a good day?"

"It was good, yes." Until I learned of the attempted murder. The subject of Christmas is as good as any. "And you're going to stay open during the holidays?"

"We always have, offer an early dinner for guests, and then have our own later. There will be a lot of cooking and baking."

"Let me know if I can help."

Maxine exchanges a look with her husband. They are clearly aware that it's a tricky subject for me. "That's very kind of you. Whatever you're comfortable with."

"It will be different from anything before, and certainly different from where I expected to be...but I'm happy to be here." That, at least, is true.

"We're happy to have you. Let's hope Mr. Roman will be okay, and we can all put this behind us."

I hope that too, so much—for Annabel, for her brother, and for Kelli's peace of mind. It's about time.

Kelli knocks on my door later that night. It's close to ten, and I wonder if she's only now coming home, or if she wanted to spend some time by herself.

"Hey. Long day," I say. "Do you have any news from Marc?"

"It's too early to say." She sounds bone tired. "They're still processing evidence from the scene, and we got the man's description out. I guess now we pray." Kelli sits down on the side of the bed, shoulders hunched. I'm startled to realize she's crying. I've been relying on her steadfast support, her strength, so much that I didn't realize how close she was to her own breaking point.

"You'll find him. You figured out what happened...what Lucas and his friends did."

That one is a difficult subject for both of us, given the involvement of my niece Fiona and her friends. They managed to pull their lives back together in the aftermath, but Kelli and I both know there was intent, not only to get justice, but revenge.

"Yes, we'll find him, but will it do any good? I'm so tired of this crap." She straightens with a sigh. "We know it's him behind all of this, yet we have to tap-dance around him. People get life for a lot less. He always has a scapegoat, or someone to cover for him."

I wish I could tell her something to change her mind. Back at home, Lucas Gavin's parents practically owned the town, controlling the majority of local jobs. If Gavin senior was inappropriate with an employee, if junior took things too far at a frat party, who would stop them?

But things aren't the same anymore, even back home. The Gavins have gotten a lot quieter since their son's text messages came out. Kelli helped make that happen.

With the latest developments, it should be obvious to everyone that Dan Emmett has no good intentions. I put my arm around her and pull her close.

"I love you," I say. Because it's easy, and it's true.

"I love you too. And I'm sorry. You have a lot on your mind as well. I didn't even ask you how the job went."

I wonder if she talked to her parents before she came up here.

"Pretty well. I think it's a good fit. But my worries are hardly on the same scale."

"Would you like to go see your family for Christmas?"

I take a long time to answer because there's no good, clean way.

"I think the question is rather would they like to see me? To be honest I've done my best to avoid thinking about it."

"You could call them...read the room?"

"The room will be chilly. No one will say I can't come, but I'm not sure I'd feel welcome either."

"Whatever you decide. If you want to go, I'll come with you."

I give her a quizzical look. "I thought you'd never want to set foot into town again."

"If it's important to you, I'll do it. Otherwise, we try to keep it relaxed around here."

My turn to sigh. "I'm all for relaxed."

I do feel like a coward given the fact that I woke my happily remarried ex-husband in the middle of the night but haven't spoken to my parents in weeks. The arrogant and likely criminal man from out of town is not the only problem.

❧

He definitely is a problem though. I'm more angry than scared when I greet the participants for the afternoon tour, realizing he's standing there next to a family of five.

"I'm sorry, sir, I can't find your name on my list," I say, keeping my tone polite, but icy. I remember what Kelli said—he doesn't get his hands dirty in public. He's not going to do anything to me with the group around.

"That's fine. I made a modest donation to the city's library and tourist office. A pleasant lady named Sally told me I could join. She says you have fascinating stories to tell."

I can see the other participants' gazes, ranging from intrigued to impatient. He's trying to rattle me, and of course, Kelli. I won't give him that satisfaction. As long as he's walking around with us, he can't get to Annabel, or Marc. Or anyone.

"Is that so? Well, in that case, welcome to the tour. I hope you'll enjoy."

We take the same route, and I make sure not to turn my back to him.

To my relief, he's quiet. No inappropriate questions or comments on my eating habits or figure.

When we come to the lighthouse, I'm relieved that Eddie Burton is there to greet us today.

Like the last time, I stay with the ones less fond of heights, and the parents of small children.

"You're not coming up?" Emmett asks, sounding disappointed.

"No." I don't think I owe him an explanation.

To my dismay, one of the young fathers tells me, "I think we're fine down here if you want to go up. We'll just wait until you come down if you want to point out certain features?"

Emmett's eyes light up. "I'd love that."

I don't want to prolong this endlessly, so I give in. A few other members of the tour join us, and we enter the lighthouse to go up the stairs. Emmett stays close behind me, I notice. Only for me to hear, he mumbles, "Don't you think the old guy who guards this place would love a donation too?"

"Not everything and everyone is for sale." I keep my voice low as well.

"You'd be surprised. What, you aren't afraid of me? I can only imagine the stories Detective Jameson has told you. I can assure you none of them are true."

"You don't really care about the history and features of the lighthouse, do you?" I'm still new to the job. Maybe I shouldn't risk any complaints he might make to Sally, but I can't help it.

"What if I do? The thing you should know about me is that I have influence," He boasts. It could be a thinly veiled threat too, probably both. "I can make your little tour become famous overnight. For all the wrong, or the right reasons. You wouldn't want to be the reason the town goes bankrupt after they just welcomed you?"

Here we go. I do understand how Kelli hates him with every fiber of her being.

"Oh, for Christ's sake, let's just do this, okay?"

"Thank you, Ms. Burke."

The others have caught up, and I force a smile for their sake as I start to explain the different parts of the building.

On the gallery, I keep my distance from Emmett. I know he's aware, and enjoying making me uncomfortable, but it's all I can do at the moment.

"And this woman was the last lighthouse keeper before it became a museum."

"What an intriguing tale. There's no hint of a romance with anyone in town?"

"I didn't think you were interested in romance. After all, you have influence."

He laughs at that. "Touché. But I'm actually quite romantic. I believe in soulmates. Don't you, Mrs. Burke?"

"I believe we should get going. It's going to rain soon."

"You're right. It's probably dangerous out here when the material gets slippery. After you."

There's something creepy about him, beyond being a wealthy man who enjoys and exploits his privilege. He's feeding on my fear, as I walk back down in front of him.

"We're going to have a snack at *The Sand Dollar Inn*, isn't that right?"

At the bottom of the circular staircase, I turn to him.

"It is part of the tour. If I were you, I wouldn't attend though."

The polite smiling mask only slips for a split-second.

"Why would you say that? I paid for it, and then some."

"Suit yourself, Mr. Emmett."

I hope that there won't be any confrontation, though that's almost unavoidable. I don't know what to do.

It occurs to me that spending all afternoon with the tour, being seen by multiple tourists is giving him the perfect alibi, in case he had anything—else?—planned.

Maxine's eyes widen when she sees him sitting at the table. I get up and take her aside, out of the group's earshot.

"I'm so sorry," I blurt out. "I didn't know...He paid Sally a lot of money, and I had to take him. Could you distract them for a second while I call Kelli?"

She nods grimly. "Of course. Are you all right?"

"He didn't touch me, or anyone, for that matter. Just a lot of talking. Please, be careful."

"Don't worry. I'll take care of it."

I step out of the room to call Kelli, but my call goes to voicemail. I try her desk at the station next. A Detective Heller picks up. Should I tell him...? I don't want her to get the wrong idea. Nothing happened, but she did say to call 911 should he set foot into the inn.

"I'd like to speak to Detective Jameson if it's at all possible. I'm Merin Burke."

"She's busy right now. Is it urgent?"

The room where the guests are about to have their pie and beverage, is still quiet.

"Actually, no. It's fine. I'm sorry I disturbed you."

I hurry back to my group, only to find that neither Emmett nor Maxine are there. At the front door, I hear raised voices.

"We told you not to come here again. Now, Mr. Emmett, leave before I call the police."

"The real police or your daughter?" he scoffs. "She's insane. You better worry about her."

Maxine yanks the door open. Shaking his head, he leaves. I realize I'm trembling. This could have gone wrong in various ways.

"I'm so sorry."

"Don't worry about it," she says. "I understand. I will talk to Sally as well, and I'm sure she's going to give back that donation. We don't know exactly what he got away with, but I don't like him. No one calls my daughter a liar in my house."

I'm not sure which was the last straw, but all of a sudden, the room swims before my eyes. Maybe it's looking at a parent who stands up for their daughter, no matter what.

"Oh, sweetie," she says and embraces me.

"I need to go back in there."

"You can take a moment. I'll get them their pie, and you go back in when you're ready."

"Thank you." I find the closest bathroom to wash my face and spend a few embarrassing minutes before I put the smile back into place and join the group to finish my workday.

Chapter Twelve

Kelli

Heller and I check out an anonymous tip regarding the weapon used in the attempted murder.

The caller manipulated their voice, claiming they saw a man clad in black dump a knife in a public garbage bin. I'm willing to believe it's either a hoax or a false lead fed to us by Emmett, but when we get to work with gloved hands, it doesn't take us long to unearth the steak knife, blood crusted on the blade and handle.

This will go to a lab out of town for a quicker turnaround.

My phone rings. Given the fact that we're both still wearing the latex gloves, I let it go to voicemail. The tip panning out is a small victory. Given what we're up against, I'll take it. With a little luck, there's DNA, even blood other than Marc's.

He's still weak, but he'll pull through. Another victory. This time, Emmett won't get away. As long as the case is moving along, there's no reason to pull me off it.

The phone rings again when we are back in the car. It only takes a couple of minutes worth of conversation with my mother to destroy my hopeful mood.

It doesn't get better when I'm back home, and we continue said conversation.

"Are you out of your mind?"

"Kelli, you're out of line."

Mom might have a point, but I need to voice my frustration and fear. Unfortunately, she and Merin are the nearest targets.

"How much clearer do I have to spell it out for you? He targets his victims, stalks them, then he kidnaps and abuses them. Annabel Roman got away within an inch of her life. There's at least one woman dead, that we know of. He's been laughing in our faces, and you let him in the house?"

"It's my fault," Merin says, looking dejected. "He told me Sally said it was okay. I should have known. Maxine asked him to leave, and he did."

"You should have waited for me. What if he'd gotten violent, with either one of you, or one of the guests?"

"That's not the M.O., right?"

"It's not your job to think about either. I can't believe you. Both of you."

"I believe you made your point." Dad has joined us in the living room. His calm tone does nothing to my state of alarm.

"It's not about being right. He's an abuser and a murderer!"

"He wasn't going to do anything in front of this many witnesses," Merin defends herself. "You said it yourself, he's smart. He got away with a lot. I thought I might overhear anything that might help. I don't know. He said that if he couldn't come on the tour, he'd make sure the town goes bankrupt. Considering what you told me about him, I didn't think he was bluffing." Merin has raised her voice, too. "I cannot lose another home. This is too much."

She flees for her room, and for several seconds, all of us stand in stunned silence.

"You go fix it," Mom tells me. "After that, I'd like to talk to you about something."

I'm not optimistic that it will be a quick and easy fix.

I screwed up.

She opens the door to me right away.

"Can I come in?"

Merin looks as if she has to think about that for a moment, before she steps aside.

"I'm sorry," I say. "I shouldn't have yelled at you."

She doesn't dispute that statement.

"You know we weren't kidding when we said you always have a home here. No one's going to kick you out because of Emmett's threats."

"Maybe not."

"Can you forgive me?" Yesterday she said she loved me. I want to slap myself.

"That's not what this is about. Of course I forgive you. You're under a lot of stress, I get it. I had no choice but to take him on the tour. He paid. He's not accused of any crime at this point. What was I supposed to do?"

"I'm sorry. I'll talk to Sally. In fact, I'm going to talk to a lot of people, starting tomorrow. No one around here is obligated to serve him. Once he finds that out, he might even leave by himself."

"Is he worth all of that?"

"What do you mean?"

"You're risking your job, and your livelihood again." She raises tear-filled eyes at me. "We all did that, stand up for the right thing, put it all on the line. George is happy. I know you can't let this go, but I'm just not that strong or courageous. Don't you remember? I came here because I had nowhere else to go. I always wait until my back's against the wall, and even then I mess up. Perhaps I should leave."

"Merin, no."

This shouldn't come as a shock, but the depth of her grief and self-reproach feels staggering. After everything we've said, experienced together, she's still taking the blame even when it doesn't belong. I can't let that stand.

"Okay, let's be very clear. You could and should have said no to him, but Mom took care of it, and everyone's fine. It's fine. I'll handle the rest tomorrow. No one will deny that he's been crossing lines. I shouldn't have yelled at you. I was worried—that's not a good enough excuse. Merin, you are the strongest person I know!"

Merin gives me a dismissive shrug.

"It's true! I can't even begin to imagine what it's been like for you, losing your home, having to deal with ignorance all around you, even from loved ones. I don't know that I would have had the courage to come out. You could have blamed it all on George and stayed under the radar, find a new house, a new husband."

"No, I couldn't," she whispers. "It's not because I was brave. It's because I couldn't stop thinking about you. I wanted to be with you."

"And you made it happen. Please, don't mix things up. If there's something to repair with your parents and your sister, you will when the time is right. If not, that's on them. Meanwhile, I need you to stay away from Emmett. He'll exploit every possible weakness, and..."

"I am yours?"

The hint of a smile warms my heart.

"Yes, you are mine." I lean in to kiss her softly, and she meets me all the way.

Whatever Mom wanted to talk about, she'll have to wait a little bit longer.

❧

I don't get to talk to her in the morning either, though I trust that they'll see Merin at breakfast and know we cleared the air between us.

I'm on a mission, and I want to do it early, before Heller comes in. Before any more awkward phone calls happen.

I knock on my boss's door, and he calls me in.

"Good morning, sir. Do you have a minute?"

"Sure, take a seat." His demeanor is friendly, though I'm sure he wonders if he'll regret saying yes so quickly. It's not up to me.

"Dan Emmett showed up at my parents' place again even though they asked him the other day to stay away. He also joined a guided tour..." I wince at that, realizing how it sounds without the context. "My partner is the tour guide. He made more threats, to get her fired, to mess with local tourism."

He listens closely, his face impassive. When I've finished, he asks,

"Do you want to file a restraining order?"

"I thought about it, but his lawyers are just going to have a field day. Let me bring him in, make him see that he's not above the law."

"And you think his lawyers are going to be fine with that? I hate to tell you this, but he sounds like a nuisance. Your parents are running a private business. They have the right to serve or turn away whomever they want. He might not like it, but that's the way it is. If anyone's in physical danger, we come back to that restraining order. Otherwise, you need to let it go."

"Are you ready to tell Annabel and Marc Roman the same thing? Let's at least put a tail on him."

"What judge would sign off on that? The man might be an asshole, but he has the right to travel and join a guided tour if he wants to learn about pirates. I'm sorry, but my hands are tied."

"Wow. I thought this was different."

"What are you talking about?"

I shouldn't. He's already impatient. Merin is right, I gain nothing if I risk my job again. This would all be my doing, and I can't live under my parents' roof forever. I have no excuse.

"Nothing. I'm sorry."

"Heller will be primary, and I promise you I'll make sure he has all the resources he needs."

"I said I'm—"

"You finish up the report on those robberies. Go," he dismisses me. "If Emmett turns out to be a danger to anyone, he'll be held accountable."

I can't help thinking those are nothing more than words. I've heard them before. Nothing changes.

Not this time, though. I wasn't kidding when I told Merin there were people I needed to talk to.

I keep my head down for the rest of the day, paperwork, phone calls, finishing up the report on the robberies, as ordered. The suspect we arrested confessed. With the combined damage he did in the break-ins, and the stolen car he started to sell off piece by piece, probation is probably not in his future.

Usually, I'd be fine with that. He's a bratty twenty-something who was out to make a quick buck.

But Emmett, sitting in his penthouse office with a 360 degrees view, luring women into his web. Women who disappear. The way the case went...I blame much of it on my old boss, but it turns out Emmett's reach goes much further.

I'm afraid it's not over.

For Annabel, or for me. All of a sudden it doesn't seem like such a bad idea to get Merin out of town over the coming holidays. My promise to accompany her might have been premature, because already, the supervisor on my new job is watching me.

Am I going at this all wrong?

◦◦◦

It's not petty, but a necessary precaution when I head over to the library to speak to Sally. To my relief, Merin isn't here.

"Maxine already called me," Sally says. "I'm sorry. He sounds like an unpleasant fellow. That donation was too good to be true."

"What exactly did he say to you? About Merin...or me?"

"He didn't mention you at all, just said that he wanted to join the tour and was willing to pay more than the usual price. In fact, he paid twice of what the other participants' fees were all together."

I barely hold back the impulse to snort. That's not even pocket money to Emmett.

"Yes, the best would be to give it back. All of it. Mom kicked him out before the snack. I can make up the difference."

"Don't worry about it, but thanks for warning me."

"You're welcome."

I leave, satisfied to know that by tomorrow, there won't be many businesses in town to serve Dan Emmett. Sally's a bit of a busybody, and that will work to my advantage.

◦◦◦

Retaliation is swift: When I leave work the next day, a couple of reporters are waiting for me. I don't know them, but they identify themselves as employees of the local newspaper, one with a camera, the other one brandishing a notebook.

"Detective Jameson, Mr. Emmett claims that you're waging a vendetta against him. Do you have any comment?"

I open my mouth and close it again. This is what he wants, baiting me into saying something that would cost me my job. Then I'd have even less leverage. It's not going to happen. "No comment. Thank you."

"Is it true that you were fired from your earlier job for not pursuing other suspects in the murder of Chloe Banks?"

"No comment." I rush to my car, and to my relief, they remain at a distance, speaking to each other in rapid, hushed tones. I can only hope this is not the beginning of worse things to come. I still want to look at homes with Merin, soon, but tonight I'll talk to her about getting out of town for a bit. We don't even have to see her family. I need to know she's safe. It's no coincidence that Emmett showed up for the tour.

It's a warning.

Chapter Thirteen

T hings become a whole lot more complicated in a heartbeat when I walk inside the inn and go upstairs to realize my parents have dinner guests. The table is set for six—they put a plate for me.

"Hi, Kelli! How are you?"

"I'm fine, thanks. How are you?" Next to Fiona Collins sits Merin's mother. Her greeting is a lot more cool and sober when we shake hands. In a heartbeat I realize that this was what they wanted to talk about yesterday.

Merin's stiff posture tells me she didn't know about the visit either. It was done with good intentions, no doubt about it, but we have yet to see if it will do any good. Sam keeps close to her, curled up next to her chair. *Good dog.* He has always picked up on his humans' emotions, and I'm sure he senses that she's upset.

"Kelli, you'll sit down to eat with us?" Dad asks.

"Yes, of course. If you'll just excuse me for a minute?"

It takes me more than a minute to get out of my clothes, into a quick hot shower, and into an after-work outfit. In my mind, I'm cursing most of the time. If Fiona and her grandmother stay longer, there's no way I can whisk Merin away.

I understand the general idea, and if Merin's mother is willing to keep the lines of communication open, the timing doesn't matter. Almost.

What a mess.

I pull my hair into a ponytail, grimace at my reflection in the mirror and head back down.

Mom, Dad, and Fiona do most of the talking. If anything, it's a relief to see that the teenage girl is doing so well after a traumatic experience. Merin's mother is polite, but clearly out of her element. I admit I don't have much sympathy. She'd rather Merin stay in a marriage that didn't satisfy her, or her husband, than be honest and authentic. Happy.

I know I need to work harder to be the partner she deserves, but in our relationship, we found something real, something that goes far beyond sexual intimacy. Even if that matters, too.

"I can only stay for a couple of days," she says. "I'll have to be back before Christmas. The dinner will be at our house."

"Mom says it's okay if I stay longer." Fiona seems excited about the prospect. "If you'll have me."

"Of course," Mom and I say in unison. "Any family and friends of Merin are always welcome," she adds.

Merin takes a sip of her wine, and then another. I can sympathize. Silence ensues. Everyone is looking down at their plates, except I catch Merin's gaze and give her what I hope is an encouraging smile.

"We were wondering if you ever wanted to come home."

Merin's chair scrapes across the floor. I'm not the only one to wince.

"Mom! They fired me. I live and work here now. Kelli and I are going to move into a new place together."

I'm glad she made that clear.

"Really? That's cool," Fiona says. "The landscape is really awesome. Must be great in the summer."

Merin's mom looks like she wants to say something, but she bites her tongue.

"I'm sure there's a lot to love about where you're from too." Mom is diplomatic, Fiona less so.

"Lots of farms and fields, not much to do. At least you have the city nearby. We can go sometime, right, Merin?"

Even she and I haven't been to the city much. I can tell she's overwhelmed. I'm getting there. Now I have even more people to worry about, and Emmett isn't showing any signs of stopping his scheming. Damn it. I almost forgot about the reporters. I can only hope they decided they didn't get enough of a soundbite and drop the footage of me altogether.

"Maybe," Merin hedges. "I'm going to be pretty busy with the tours, but I suppose you could come along...if you're interested." My heart breaks at the pleading tone that's not for her niece, but her mother.

"Why don't we let you have some time to get settled in, and you take Merin's tour the day after tomorrow? I hear it's great."

"Yes. Let's call it a night soon," Merin agrees with Mom. Everyone's relief is palpable.

There's more wine and awkward conversation before the newcomers retreat to their rooms, and I follow Merin to hers. I'll have to have a word with Mom and Dad, but that can wait until tomorrow.

I didn't expect Merin to start laughing the moment we close the door behind ourselves.

"Are you okay? What did I miss?"

She's tired, and tipsy. Still.

"I think that didn't go quite as your parents had planned." She's still cracking up.

"I'd agree, but that's funny?"

"Oh, I don't know, but I'd rather laugh than cry. Fiona staged the whole thing, by the way. She found the number of the inn, called, and I guess they were in cahoots together."

"In cahoots?" I have to laugh too. "Okay. But your mom came. It's a start, isn't it?"

"To tell me I should come back. I'm sure they're talking about me in town. No, wait, I know."

"Probably. You've been around long enough now to know that gossip isn't a rarity here either."

"Not that kind of gossip. Everyone knows we are together, and I haven't seen anyone break a window."

"Speaking of windows, remember, we have an appointment for a house tomorrow. Perhaps they want to come?"

"I'd rather you and I go first."

"Of course."

It still bothers me that we can't get out of town. Maybe a change of perspective is what we need more than a change of location.

My hope is that when Merin's mother goes home, Merin will stop thinking that she wasn't brave enough, or just plain not enough. And that the same will be true for me.

Merin

I can't even begin to process all my mixed feelings. My mother
actually came to see me. She's not going to stay over Christmas, because there's a party to host, but this is nothing small.
Dad, Ellen, and her husband Drew are still processing as well, I
guess.

I'm grateful for Kelli who seems to know instinctively what
I need, and ready to give it—even when she, too, has a lot to
wrestle with. After a good night's sleep in her arms, I feel less
caught off guard, more ready to tackle whatever it is I need to do,
to say to make my family understand I'm not confused, wrong,
or sick.

In fact, I'm healing. Whole, for the first time.

Kelli leaves for work, and I head down to the breakfast room,
stopping cold when I realize it's only Mom and Maxine sitting
at a table, talking.

"That must have been a big surprise," I hear Maxine say.

This is not a good idea. I continue my eavesdropping anyway.

"It wasn't for you?" Mom sounds genuinely curious.

"To be honest, no. We were wondering when Kelli was going
to talk to us. After we walked in on her and the exchange student kissing, we sat her down for that awkward parent-teenager
talk...not because the student was a girl, but because we wanted

them to be safe. Look on the bright side, you don't have to do that."

"No one had any objections, in your church, anywhere? You just allowed it?"

This is where I should go in and pretend I never heard anything of that conversation.

"It's not a matter of allowing it. We were aware, of course, that some people are kinder than others." There's an edge to Maxine's voice, and I'm torn between wanting to hug her, and defend my mother. She's not a bigot. I know that, right?

"You don't think it's wrong? Don't you want grandchildren? I'm just afraid that it's all George's influence, that he talked her into something, and took away her chance at—"

I storm into the room before she has the chance to say "being normal."

"It has nothing to do with grandchildren, Mom. George and I made choices because we were afraid, and I know now that we had every reason to be. What if Kelli and I had children? Would you even want to see them?" I'm getting far, far ahead of myself.

"Merin, I want you to be happy. George, he seemed like such a good man. We had no idea!"

"He *is* a good man. I am happy now, and so is he. We both deserve it."

Maxine quietly leaves us, and I sit down at the table.

"Mom, you can't change or ignore this. I am who I am." Another couple of guests enter the room, and I lower my voice. "I love you."

"I love you too," she says, and I release the breath I was holding. "Of course. Do you really think I would have come, and Ellen would allow Fiona to stay by herself if we didn't care about you?"

"Fiona's of age now."

"Her parents are still paying for her tuition and housing. I know we need to talk. Maybe we can't do all of it at this moment, but I wanted to see you. See how you are."

It's still too much. I have to do my job, the one I just got. Barely blinking back more tears, I say, "That means a lot. And I want to talk to you. I've wanted that for a long time, but I'm afraid I need to get something to eat now. I need to be at work soon."

"Sure." She gets up to join me at the buffet, and Maxine returns, a relieved smile on her face. I'll have to have a word with her too.

"Let me know if there's anything else you need."

"Everything looks delicious, thank you."

They are polite, but there's still residual tension. Maybe there should be. Mixed in with my relief is knowing that some parents don't take that long to come to the same conclusion.

⁂

Emmett doesn't show up another time, so I can spend the day in peace, hoping the same is true for Kelli. After coming back from my tour, I don't go home right away but wait for her in town so she can pick me up for the house viewing. It's a bit off the beaten path, but not too far from town or the inn.

I'm excited when we get out of the car to walk to the front door. Kelli's gaze is on me, affectionate, and for a moment I can make myself believe that all those challenges don't exist. We're just like any couple looking for a place to live.

The realtor shakes hands with both of us.

"We spoke on the phone," she says to Kelli. "I look forward to showing you the place. It's perfect for two, but there's room if you wanted to expand." She winks and turns to unlock the door, Kelli and I sharing an amused gaze—until I remember Mom's comment to Maxine, about grandchildren.

Was that ever in the future? George and I didn't even talk about it. What if Kelli wants children? Do I? I might still resent him a little, for entirely irrational reasons. I could have spoken up earlier. I could have left, but I didn't, safe in denial until I wasn't.

Now's not the time. One step at a time, right? That much is still true.

Chapter Fourteen

Kelli

I can tell Merin is in love. Having some family members here at this moment is complicated, but she's handling it well. Once we've stepped into the charming little house, I know she's forgotten all about those worries, at least for a moment.

I can't.

Roger called earlier to tell me that Emmett is planning to mount a media campaign surrounding a new project of his, and Annabel's re-emergence. But he's still in town, waiting for...what? I didn't get the green light for surveillance, but I drove past the place he rented. I didn't stop.

All of this is still on my mind as I walk with Merin and the realtor through the partly furnished family home. It could be ours. The layout is a bit old-fashioned, but we could always tackle renovations later.

"The previous owners did some work upstairs," the realtor says. "These houses usually don't come with an *en suite*, but this property has one. That, and more closet space than you'd think."

"My old house didn't have one," Merin says, then stops herself as if she's crossed some line. I was in that bedroom when I shouldn't have been. Perhaps she remembers that too.

We could fill the cabinets with porcelain dishes like the Warrens did. I can imagine it. It would be a nice place to come home to.

There's a deck in the back with a view of the water.

We can make this happen. All of it.

We haven't signed anything yet, but the realtor warned us—other people are interested in a romantic home like this, and we have days, not longer, to decide.

Nevertheless, we want to celebrate having begun the search. This time, we dine at an upscale restaurant in town called The Schooner. They promise excellent seafood, and the selection of cocktails is pretty appealing too.

"It never stops, does it?" Merin remarks, bringing the subject back to the matter at hand. "I don't know if I can make a decision that quickly."

"You liked it, right? And we both have an income. I have some savings that could go towards a down payment, and the bank will figure out the rest."

"That easy?" She laughs.

"It can be. As long as you still want to live with me in this town."

"You have no idea how much I want that, and you're right, we can't stay at your parents' forever. But buying? That's a big responsibility."

"You did it with George, right?"

"Yes, but..." She stops, probably aware that there's no easy, good way to end this sentence. "Forget what I said. I still have some of the insurance money, and when I left the school, I cashed in my retirement fund. Yes, I loved that house. And I love you. If you want it, I'm with you all the way. Please bear with me when I slip back into 'old Merin' who thought nothing would ever change. A lot has changed, and that's a good thing."

"I agree. I never saw myself in a place like that...until now. I love you too. I want to take on a big responsibility with you—and I promise you, we won't take on more than we can handle."

"Ladies, good evening. I didn't expect you here tonight. Should I be worried?"

I'm on my feet before Emmett even finished the sentence. "What the hell are you doing here?"

"Getting dinner," he says with a jovial smile. "Same thing you two seem to be doing. Anything you can recommend?"

"I recommend you leave immediately. Leave this place, leave town. You have a business to run, don't you? And don't ever come near my family again."

It's a heartfelt statement, possibly a mistake. I can tell from the calculating gaze.

"You're still the same pitiful, paranoid woman I met five years ago. Annabel is alive and well, so nothing you kept accusing me of can be true. I didn't murder her, obviously, and I didn't murder Chloe—in fact I'm still paying her mother's monthly mortgage."

I can feel the color drain from my face. I didn't know that. He keeps in touch, keeps exerting power. It shouldn't surprise me. He had the power to have me sent to a tiny town far away from home, for something that wasn't a simple assignment.

"So, if you'll excuse me now, I'm going to enjoy the charming small-town cuisine. *Bon appétit*." He walks away, but I'm not willing to let this go. It's too close, too dangerous for everyone I care about.

"Mr. Emmett, please wait a minute." Changing tactics. It's a last-minute resort, but a little groveling works with men like him, even if it's fake. Their inflated ego can't tell the difference.

"Detective. I think we've said everything."

"Let's meet," I say. "Let's have a conversation. Maybe...I do owe you an apology." I'm glad we're a few steps away from where Merin still sits at the table, regarding us anxiously. Maybe she's mad at me, too.

"Is that so?"

"I want to understand what happened, with Annabel, and Chloe, and move on. I think that would serve both of us. How about tomorrow for a late lunch?"

"Are you paying? No, I'm joking, I have an idea what the paycheck of a local cop looks like."

Of course. He just can't help himself, yet, every word is calculated to make the most impact. I don't take the bait.

"We can do it here," he adds. "I'm not sure you will like the truth."

"The truth is all I need. Thank you. Two o'clock?"

"I'll be there."

I return to our table and sit back across from Merin.

"What was that?" Her tone is quiet, but she's definitely unhappy with my actions.

"I'm not sure yet, but he's not going anywhere. There must be a reason, especially with Annabel and Marc leaving town."

"Didn't your boss say you're supposed to stay away from that case? You might be risking your job."

"Not if Emmett agreed to meet with me. It will just be lunch, just talking."

"Are you—?" Merin stops herself, reconsidering her words. "This isn't good, Kelli. I think we should keep our distance."

"We can't if he isn't doing the same. Believe me, I know him. He's going to trip up at some point, make a mistake."

"What if he doesn't and you lose your job? What if it takes another five years?"

She sounds frustrated, and I can't blame her. Given everything that has happened in less than a year, this sounds like a long scary period of time. Indefinitely. It's scaring me too, but I don't see any alternative.

"That's not going to happen. We need to be on the safe side."

Our dishes arrive. Merin frowns at hers.

"I'm not sure I'm hungry anymore."

"No, don't let him ruin this." I steal a fry off her plate.

"Hey. You have your own."

My plan worked, though. I got her to smile.

"We have to eat, and we have to pay for this now. I'm not willing to let perfectly good food to waste. On the bright side, as long as he's here, he's not doing anything criminal."

"I wish I had your optimism," Merin says. At least, leaving the premises is no longer an option, and we continue our dinner in relative peace.

⁂

"You're really going to meet with him?" she asks, late at night. Neither of us has gotten much sleep. The sound of the sea, for once, doesn't help. The angry crashing of waves against the sand is too much like my mood, my anger for Emmett, and for myself because I keep getting into this kind of situation.

But how can I let it go?

"I have to. See if it can shake something loose."

"What if someone else took Annabel? Or she was in hiding the whole time, and had an accident that made her lose her memory?"

She doesn't offer a third version—the idea that Annabel might lie. There's too much evidence against it, the obvious trauma she's lived through. In my experience, people want to

115

brush off stories like hers because they're uncomfortable. But discomfort is irrelevant in this case.

"The boat is non-descript. It was rented from a company in the city harbor, but no one remembers anything," I recall from the report. "Or they're not telling."

"What if someone else did it?" Merin repeats, her tone slightly sharper. "Yes, he's an asshole, and he likes to control and insult people, but someone else might have done this. Murdered the other woman. Unfortunately, there are a few people capable of this, some of them teenagers."

"Emmett might have been a frat boy at some point, but he's moved on to bigger things."

"Okay then," Merin uses a more conciliatory tone as she snuggles into my arms.

"What does that mean?"

"It means okay, I'll help you with whatever you need."

"No, wait a minute." This is not good. "You're not supposed to—"

"We made a pretty good team last time, right? I promise you I'm not looking to do anything stupid, but you're already going out on a limb here. I'll support you any way I can. Because I love you, and..." I wait as she struggles for words. "Because none of us did enough to support Erica."

She's not wrong about that. At least, in uncovering the chains of events that led to the rapist's death, we got people in town to take a good hard look at their stances. The Gavins aren't that all-powerful anymore, but Erica McQuade paid a hefty price.

"Fiona says the McQuades moved. They're still in touch. Erica is doing much better."

"That's good." What I'm not saying is that everyone seems to be doing better once they leave that town. Of course, we have to deal with Emmett here and now, so I don't have that much talking room. "And thank you. I swear I won't let this take over our lives. We are both ready for peaceful times."

"Yes, we are."

I brush my hand over her hair, the repetitive motion both sensual and calming. With the air cleared between us, we both manage to fall asleep.

Merin

I find it hard to concentrate on something as mundane as breakfast knowing what Kelli is up to today. My task is easy, just keep my phone charged at all times. I have only one tour in the morning. After that I'll show Mom and Fiona around town...while Kelli is having lunch with a man she assumes has killed two women.

And none of that seems to have an impact on her appetite. I find myself smiling despite the challenges ahead.

"Maxine tells me you really liked that house?" Mom sounds wistful. It's not that I didn't want to tell her about it, or that I got into many details with Maxine.

"Yes, it's beautiful. I could see us living there. We have a couple of days to perhaps see something else and decide."

"The houses are so cute," Fiona says. "I could come visit you. Maybe I could even get a summer job."

"We'll run that by Ellen once you're home," Mom reminds her.

"I already visited the university. It's not that far from here, only about two hours."

It seems like a different reality, Mom, Fiona and her plans, and the danger men like Emmett pose, on the other hand...But we're no strangers to megalomaniacal men. Lucas Gavin's parents bought the silence of elected officials and law enforcement.

"You really don't want to come back?"

"I can't. I don't have a job there."

Before I can elaborate, Mom says, "You could move in with us until you find something. The sheriff's office has changed completely, except for Woodward. I'm sure Kelli could find work there."

I seek Kelli's gaze, and I know she's as shocked as I am. Not that I'd want to move back in with my parents. Mom acknowledging that we're together, in it for the long run, is a huge step.

"We could always come to visit," Kelli suggests.

I'm even more in love with her. The fog is finally lifting from my life, and I can sort out the lingering guilt and regrets...once that other problem is solved.

Chapter Fifteen

Kelli

I'm early, but Emmett already sits in a booth at the diner. He gets up to greet me, all polite gentleman now. That's how he lures in the women. I don't shake his hand, and we sit down. Immediately, a waitress arrives to hand us our menus. I choose a shrimp salad, he goes with the surf & turf. I wish I could drink, but we both stick with water.

"Okay, Ms. Jameson, this is your moment. I'm not sure what you hope to achieve but have at it. You and I both know that you can't use anything you record with the wire you're wearing, in court."

"I'm not wearing a wire. This isn't official. I just wanted to talk."

"So you keep saying, but what would it help? You must move on with or without my blessing, Kelli. I won."

My stomach lurches. I don't know if it's him going from "Detective" to "Ms" to using my first name in this intimate tone, or his definite statement. *I won.* It means he got away, and he's not going to stop. Or at least, that's what he thinks. Not on my watch. Not if I have anything to say about it.

"You might be right about that. I've been called off the case. Other cops will keep an eye on you, maybe, until the pile of files

121

on their desks gets too high. I guess this is it. Will you at least tell me why? How you pulled it off?"

He hesitates, a faraway look on his face, and I almost think *I got him*.

Our food arrives.

"My, this looks delicious," Emmett beams at the waitress who blushes. "Let's eat first, Kelli, shall we? I promise I'll tell you what you want to know, but I don't want this to get cold."

I don't know that I can contain my hate for this man, his murderous entitlement, much longer. I do want to remind him that there will be consequences if he ever comes near Merin or my parents again. I want to threaten him. I do none of those things because I know patience will pay off. I might be pathetic and hopeless, but I've tried everything else.

"I just want closure," I say.

"I understand. This steak is one of the best I've ever had. Remarkable how much talent is hidden in small towns like this. And it's peaceful, don't you think? I might be looking at investing in a permanent home."

For someone who doesn't want his food to get cold he's sure talking a lot. I can't be distracted, but his statement strikes me as ridiculous. I laugh.

"No, you won't. You'd get bored."

"You might be right about that. So—what do you want to know?"

I hold his gaze, trying to suppress the shudder that wants to run down my spine. He's ready—so I must be, too.

"Why Annabel and Chloe? And why is one of them dead and the other isn't? She got away?"

"They were both attractive, and vulnerable. You understand the lure of attractive, vulnerable women, don't you, Kelli?"

I'm feeling nauseated again.

"This is not about me."

"It might not be, but there's a reason why you're here with me, and not your colleague Heller, right?"

"You want to tell me we have something in common?" Let me throw up now.

"I wouldn't go that far. I think we have...an understanding. Anyway, they were both interesting for a while. Entertaining."

"But you got bored eventually."

"You could say that," he admits. "I don't do bored very well, so I had to...sever...ties." The emphasis is not a coincidence.

"How did you do it? You had an alibi both times. I always thought it was because you wouldn't get your hands dirty, but this isn't the same as attacking Marc Roman. You wanted him out of the way. With Annabel and Chloe, it was personal. You wouldn't leave that to an employee?"

"Now you're getting far ahead of yourself. Both Annabel and Chloe enjoyed the comfort of my hospitality. They loved the luxury life but didn't understand what it takes to be worthy of the lifestyle."

"So, you taught them a lesson," I conclude.

"They were grateful. I can assure you of that."

"Annabel was missing for five years, Chloe for six weeks. What was different?" I can barely hear myself over my hammering heart. We are so close. And he's right, I probably couldn't use any of it in court, but he's admitting guilt for the first time. I can build on that.

"I got bored sooner. Look, this is interesting, but Chloe isn't talking, and Annabel doesn't even remember her name. We're finally on the same page? Some people take what they want. I'm one of them, and there's nothing you can do about it. Sad. Pathetic, for sure, but you can always say you tried. Don't feel too bad about it, Kelli. You're not the first, or the last."

"Thank you," I say.

That stops him in his tracks. His eyes narrow, a suspicious gleam in them.

"What do you mean?"

"You've confirmed everything I already knew about you, Mr. Emmett. Stay away from my family. You'll regret it if you don't."

"Funny, I didn't think you were in a position to threaten me." The jovial smile is back.

"I'm not threatening you. Just to make sure we're still on the same page." I toss a bill on the table and get up.

"What, no dessert?" he taunts.

"No, thanks. I've had enough."

I walk out of the restaurant without looking back, though his triumphant grin is burned into my memory.

The urge to throw up is still strong when I sit behind the wheel of my car. Maybe Merin had a point. This solves everything and nothing.

I take my cell phone out of the pocket of my blazer and replay the part: *Some people take what they want. I'm one of them, and there's nothing you can do about it.*

Sad. Pathetic.

We'll see.

Chapter Sixteen

I go back to work where I miraculously manage to keep my head down. I read over the police report again. Heller wrote it after Annabel washed up on the shore. I find nothing new.

To my surprise, Emmett didn't complain about my conduct again. The end of my shift rolls around. As I'm about to turn off my computer, I look up to see Heller standing in front of my desk.

"Hey," he said. "I was wondering if you'd like to go for a drink?"

It's not entirely out of nowhere. We'll have to work together for the foreseeable future. Given that I'm not particularly good at making friends, this is an opportunity I shouldn't miss, even if I was looking forward to spending time with Merin—and catching her up on the day's events.

"Sure, why not? Give me a second?"

"Of course. I'll be right outside."

I send her a short text. *Lunch went pretty well. I'll tell you later. Joining a colleague for a drink, be home soon.*

Heller waits for me in the lobby, and we walk a couple of blocks to a bar that looks fairly friendly and inviting.

It doesn't take long to go back to the shop talk. We sit at the counter, both with an order of beer and chips in front of us, when he says, "There is no freaking trace of the guy who attacked Roman's brother. He's a ghost."

"No DNA from the knife?" I expected that already.

"No, just the victim's blood. I know you think it's related to Emmett, but either way it's bad. If it was random, that guy might attack other people with a knife." I hold back the comment. There was nothing random about this. Heller acknowledges this.

"If it's not, we're dealing with a rich guy who hires goons for knife attacks. None of this is much appealing, and to be honest, I didn't think it could happen here."

"You've worked here long?" I ask, curious.

"I came back right after graduating," he confirms. "And it's never been like this."

"I hope you're not saying I'm the one who brought bad luck to the town."

He chuckles. "No, Jameson, I'm not saying that. I was telling you that you might have a point. You know him better than anyone. If we could tie the attacker to him, or the person who rented that boat..."

"The attacker, yes, but we'd have to find him first."

"No kidding."

"As for the boat, what if it was Annabel who took it, or a friend of hers? Someone who tried to do her a favor, help her?"

He shakes his head. "I'm not sure that's what happened. If a friend put her on that boat, they must have thought risking death was better than the situation she was in before. It just doesn't make sense. She was beyond lucky to make it to the coast."

"There's something about that boat."

"I agree."

He flags the bartender for another round of beers. I'm about to protest.

"Don't worry. My sister runs the cab company. She'll send someone if I ask her."

"Okay then." I raise my glass. "Thanks for not calling me sad and pathetic."

"Why would I?" he asks with a frown.

"Indeed."

❧

As much as I like to keep my circle to a small number of people I trust infinitely, this has been good. At my old job, I had to hold back a lot of the time, especially after Emmett's case became hot again. Even with the recent events, I don't have the same kind of history here, of having to pack up my things because the boss sent me to cool my heels in the middle of nowhere.

Heller's sister Dolores is driving the cab. She's friendly, but not too chatty. He lives not far from the bar we went to.

"I hear you're looking at one of the houses with a water view?" she says. "I'd move quickly if I were you. It's a seller's market right now. Our parents moved away, but they keep a summer house."

It's not such a big surprise that she knows about this already. In a town this size, word gets around. I don't mind it so much at the moment, even with the emotional roller-coaster of the day. It's been going according to plan. The more alliances I can forge, the harder it will be for Emmett to make his spiel work here.

I hope.

"We are thinking of buying it," I confirm.

"If you need any references for contractors, you can ask me or my brother."

She laughs at my expression. "What can I say, my siblings and I love this town, so most of us stayed and started one business or another."

127

"Sounds good. I'll let you know."

It's not just because of Emmett, I realize. In the past, I've only ever visited my parents for a few days without ever immersing myself much in the local culture. If I'm going to live here permanently, and it's pretty much decided, that will change. Merin made a big sacrifice. Working with Sally, she's already ahead of me.

Good choices. It's about time. In the long run, even the Gavins and their neighbors couldn't evade change altogether. I used to feel claustrophobic here, too. Everyone must adjust in some way, and with Merin by my side and the new home we're going to live in, we're off to a good start.

I go straight up to her room and knock, surprised there is no answer. Checking my cell phone, I notice that there hasn't been any communication since she answered my message. *Sure. Have fun. We'll talk later. Love you.*

She might be asleep already. I shouldn't wake her...I can't help the antsy feeling that's coming over me. Am I getting paranoid? I head over to my parents' quarters where I find them in the living room, watching TV.

"Have you seen Merin?" I ask without preamble.

"Why?" Dad asks. "Weren't you going to meet her in town?"

"She said that?"

"No, we just assumed when she didn't come in for dinner. Her only tour was this morning, and she went shopping with her mother and niece. I saw her mom earlier. Is everything okay?"

He sounds concerned now. I'm closer to terrified. "I need a key to her room, now. If I'm wrong, I'll make it up to everyone."

Without an argument, he gets up and follows me to the reception where he produces the key.

"Thank you." I don't wait, but sprint back up to the room, and unlock the door.

All of her things are there. A book sits on the table by the window. The bed hasn't been slept in.

"Merin?" I rush to the bathroom and yank the door open, pull the shower curtain aside. She's not here.

I sent a text message. *Where are you? Call me when you get this.*

Out of the corner of my eye, I see movement, and I spin around.

"It's just me," Dad says. "Did you find her? Should we get her mother and Fiona?"

The uncertainty gnaws at me. Merin's mom was just starting to accept the fact that we're a couple. I might ruin it, but I have to be sure.

"I'll talk to them. Let me know if Merin comes in. I'm going to go look for her. If all else fails, I'll file a missing persons report, but I'll start with what her family has to say."

He nods. At this moment I wish someone could tell me I was paranoid, but it looks more and more like I have reason to worry.

"Who's missing?" a voice asks from the doorway. My heart skips a beat. It's Merin, with Fiona in tow, looking confused. "Is something wrong?"

I want to go over at her and wrap her in an embrace. I want to assure her that everything is perfect now, but I can't make myself move or talk.

Merin, who is the only one who knows what I was up to earlier, takes action.

"Fiona, I'll see you tomorrow? Good night." When Fiona has left, she adds, "I'm not sure what's going on, but if you're all up for it, I wouldn't mind a night cap. Relax a bit?"

"That sounds like a great idea," Dad says, relieved. "I'll prepare something, and you'll join us when you're ready?"

"Yes. Thank you."

The door closes, and it's Merin who walks up to me, pulling me close. I'm trembling. I can't help it. Missing persons reports. Annabel Roman. Chloe Banks. A body dumped in an abandoned warehouse. Chloe had been wearing designer clothes and shoes, expensive make-up. Emmett's lawyers argued this meant he couldn't have done it. I knew it was to send a message. The luxury life that she, according to Dan Emmett, didn't deserve. The weakness.

"It's okay," Merin whispers. "I'm okay. I'm sorry, but since you said you were going out with your colleague, I took Fiona out to dinner. Mom was tired, so she went back to the inn."

"No, I'm sorry. I was just so used to you being here, I...I was stupid."

"I get it. I'd also like to hear about the conversation you had today, but since I roped your dad into that nightcap, I guess we'll go first?"

"Sure. Let's go."

When we join my parents, back in their living room, Dad has prepared a table with shot glasses and a bottle of Irish Cream Liquor.

"You want it like that? We still have some ice cream too."

The scene is enough to make me tear up. The past few months have been steadily wearing away at me. I needed this, being home with the people I love, but it's also making me more vulnerable than I'd like. Emmett's phrase about *vulnerable women* comes back to me, but I know it's all mind games and manipulation. I'm at home here, surrounded by good people. I also didn't have much for dinner.

"Ice cream sounds great," I say, aware of Merin's soft smile.

It's no longer so dire when we lie in each other's arms breathless and naked.

"You know," she whispers, "It's a great way to deal with the stress. I wish it could be just this, without the bad surprises."

"Me too. But this time, nothing happened."

"I'm so sorry I didn't answer right away. I should have known you were on edge after that lunch date."

"I forgive you, but please, don't call it a lunch date. I don't really want to talk about him anymore. I'll take precautions, that's all. With what I have, my boss has no choice but to believe me. I just need a good moment to present my case to him."

She leans in to kiss me.

Now is a moment for something different, but Emmett will feel the heat eventually. I need a little more time to make enough allies.

Then my mind shuts out everything but the beautiful woman in my arms. Tonight, the sound of the waves is gentle.

❦

The ringing of my cell phone sounds rude and obscenely loud in the stillness of the night. It takes me a few seconds to get to it, and by then, Merin is awake, looking at me with alarm.

"Jameson."

"Detective," my boss replies.

I'm wide awake, staring at the clock on the nightstand. 4:53. What the hell did Emmett do now? If he wanted to denounce me to the local press or my supervisor, why wait?

"Sir. What's going on? Something about Emmett?" I'm sure I know the answer.

"There was an intruder at Heller's house last night. He and his girlfriend were shot."

My hand goes to my mouth.

"How are they?"

"They'll pull through," he says tersely. "I need you here right now. We'll get another investigator from the county, but for now, you're primary."

"Of course. Could they give any description?"

"Heller's still in surgery. The girlfriend says the guy wore all black, but she's in shock. I have Officer Manning with them at the hospital."

"I'll join them there, and I'll come in as soon as possible," I promise, end the call, and start to dress.

"Bad news?" Merin asks, anxious.

That's mild. "My colleague and his girlfriend were shot in their house. They'll be okay, but...Damn. This has to end."

"It's sad that it had to come to this, but they'll believe you now?"

"I hope so. I'll catch up with you later and...Merin, I'd feel better if you canceled the tour for today. Stay close to the house with your mom and Fiona. I'll tell my parents the same."

"Okay." She doesn't argue. "I'll keep an eye on everyone."

"Thank you." After pulling my sweater over my head, I lean in for a kiss. That's the last comforting thing I'll get for a while.

Chapter
Seventeen

I get nothing new from Heller's girlfriend who is recovering in a hospital bed, looking pale and terrified.

"I told that to Officer Manning already. The man, he stood in the bedroom all of a sudden. Black clothes, baseball cap. He didn't say anything, just fired."

Her eyes fill with tears. I notice the bandage around her arm.

"I'm really sorry. Is there anything else you can think of?"

"Ryan tried to go for his gun, but it was too late. I thought we were both going to die!" She's sobbing now.

"I'm sorry," I say, my mind racing in various directions until it settles on one bone-chilling aspect. Emmett mentioned Heller during lunch—by name.

What is his end game? All this time I was afraid he was going to come for someone close to me, and I'm not convinced that isn't still his plan. I barely know Heller—why go after him? On the other hand, the more people believe I'm not a paranoid alarmist, that there's a case to be made against Emmett, the more dangerous for him.

"Find who did this," she pleads.

"I'll do everything I can," I promise. "I'll make sure you get an update you as soon as there's news." The gratitude shines through her tears.

I check in with Merin quickly before I head for Heller's apartment where the crime scene unit is still at work. It's not even six a.m., and I've already had enough of this day.

A knife, a gun, different weapons but a similar M.O. People were right to tell me that there's hardly ever been this much crime in town. It all began when Emmett arrived here.

⟡

I have no choice but to come clean right away. As soon as I've caught our boss up on the latest developments, I put my cell phone on his desk.

"I've been meaning to show you this, and I think it's even more important now."

"Does it have to do with Dan Emmett?" he asks, his tone reflecting exhaustion. "I'm beginning to curse the day this man set foot into town."

That's... hopeful? At least he doesn't curse the day he hired me.

"I'm afraid it does have to do with him. Look, I know it's all been circumstantial, but there was the attack on Marc Roman. The description of the attacker fits the one Heller's girlfriend gave."

"Loosely."

"True, but do you really think there's a sudden crime surge in town? Why would that be? Please, listen to this."

He does, with an impassive expression.

When the recording has ended, I say, "This is what he does. He thrives on chaos, throwing people off balance. He mentions Heller. I should have put it together earlier, but I..." Was so worried he could have gone for Merin. He still might plan to. "I need help. We need to watch him, and we need to protect the people who might be in danger from him. My partner, my parents...You might be on his list."

"It's a long shot." He looks frustrated and angry. "But given that he keeps showing up in all these places, and what happened with Heller and his girlfriend, we can't ignore this. I've told you there's an investigator coming in from the county. You'll work with them. Meanwhile, we'll put some measures in place, under the radar. You do what you have to do, but don't be obvious about it. We don't want to tip him off."

"Thank you."

I'm already on my way out when he voices my own thoughts.

"Let's get that son of a bitch."

A quick call to the hospital reveals that Heller's surgery went well. He's in recovery. I look at the report on Annabel, when she was found on the shore, the description of the boat, and a note as to its origin. I think of Heller's theory.

The boat might not have been Annabel's original choice. Someone might have rented it, left it in a place where she found it and used it for her escape? Or Emmett got his kicks out of leaving her out on the open sea to die. There's nothing much about the clothes she was wearing. If she had expensive make-up on her, it would have washed off.

Then I remember Merin saw her. Would she remember something about a dress?

Jotting down the words "designer dress" I decide to call her later. First, I want to know where Emmett's yacht is docked. One by one, the pieces will come together.

Merin

I call Sally and cancel the tour. Fortunately, she understands without me having to give her too many details.

Kelli's parents are busy with the inn today, getting decorations up and reservations up to date for the holidays. So far, my task is easy even though I'm doing it with a heavy heart, knowing Kelli is out there looking for the attacker. She does that kind of thing, jumping right into danger. She saved Fiona from Lucas Gavin's friend. Twice. Bradley was armed too, but at least he hadn't tried to kill anyone. Yet.

No, this is not helping.

I find Mom standing over her open suitcase, reminded that she's not going to stay.

"I have to go back," she says, sensing my thoughts. "I know you have your mind set on making a life here, and we must accept that...but you could come join us for Christmas. You know you'll be welcome."

"Is Kelli too?"

The other night, she didn't comment on Kelli's suggestion to go visit sometime.

"She is."

Only a second of hesitation means progress.

"That's good. But we still have to make a decision regarding the house. Perhaps we could come down early in the next year."

"Perhaps. Everyone would love to see you. Dad has been asking about you."

"He has?" I didn't realize they'd been talking every day since she arrived. "What did he say?"

"He wanted to know if you were sure about what you're doing, and if you were happy. I told him that as far as I can tell, the answer is yes to both."

"It is." I sit next to her on the bed. "I loved teaching. I loved my home, but when I realized I had to choose I didn't even have to think about it. George was right. If you get that chance, you must take it."

She looks wistful. "My parents weren't too keen on me marrying your father."

"Really?" Then again, if there was tension, I'm not sure I would have known. Before George and I became the scandal of the town, our families always kept things polite above all else.

"I might have threatened to run away with him. That helped." For some reason, we both have to laugh. It's not really that funny, because I did run away, because at the time, I had to.

"She makes me that happy," I say. "I want to be with her."

"Then it would make sense to buy that house."

"Yes, that would make a lot of sense." She leans close to hug me. I'm once again tearing up. The disturbing wake-up call we got might have been part of the reason.

As if on cue, my phone rings. Seeing that it's Kelli calling, I answer right away.

"Hey," she says. "Do you have a moment? I was wondering if you could help me with something."

When she tells me the reason for her call, I'm dumbfounded to say the least. "I'm not sure. She was wearing a dress, true, but I can't tell you if it was expensive or not. I suppose it was evidence, and they gave it back to her later? You should call her."

"Yes, I'll do that." Kelli sighs. "It was a reach. I guess I just wanted to hear your voice."

"Nothing wrong with that. How are you holding up? You left early."

"It's all in the caffeine," she says dryly.

"Any news on your partner?"

"Not in a while, but he and the girlfriend are recovering. On your end?"

"Everything is quiet," I tell her. "I can't wait for you to come home."

"Me too. See you later. I love you."

"Love you too."

I see Mom's pensive look, and I wonder if I could use the time to get more stories of rebellion out of her. It's good to finally connect over something, even though she's going home tomorrow.

Merin

I call Sally and cancel the tour. Fortunately, she understands without me having to give her too many details.

Kelli's parents are busy with the inn today, getting decorations up and reservations up to date for the holidays. So far, my task is easy even though I'm doing it with a heavy heart, knowing Kelli is out there looking for the attacker. She does that kind of thing, jumping right into danger. She saved Fiona from Lucas Gavin's friend. Twice. Bradley was armed too, but at least he hadn't tried to kill anyone. Yet.

No, this is not helping.

I find Mom standing over her open suitcase, reminded that she's not going to stay.

"I have to go back," she says, sensing my thoughts. "I know you have your mind set on making a life here, and we must accept that...but you could come join us for Christmas. You know you'll be welcome."

"Is Kelli too?"

The other night, she didn't comment on Kelli's suggestion to go visit sometime.

"She is."

Only a second of hesitation means progress.

"That's good. But we still have to make a decision regarding the house. Perhaps we could come down early in the next year."

"Perhaps. Everyone would love to see you. Dad has been asking about you."

"He has?" I didn't realize they'd been talking every day since she arrived. "What did he say?"

"He wanted to know if you were sure about what you're doing, and if you were happy. I told him that as far as I can tell, the answer is yes to both."

"It is." I sit next to her on the bed. "I loved teaching. I loved my home, but when I realized I had to choose I didn't even have to think about it. George was right. If you get that chance, you must take it."

She looks wistful. "My parents weren't too keen on me marrying your father."

"Really?" Then again, if there was tension, I'm not sure I would have known. Before George and I became the scandal of the town, our families always kept things polite above all else.

"I might have threatened to run away with him. That helped." For some reason, we both have to laugh. It's not really that funny, because I did run away, because at the time, I had to.

"She makes me that happy," I say. "I want to be with her."

"Then it would make sense to buy that house."

"Yes, that would make a lot of sense." She leans close to hug me. I'm once again tearing up. The disturbing wake-up call we got might have been part of the reason.

As if on cue, my phone rings. Seeing that it's Kelli calling, I answer right away.

"Hey," she says. "Do you have a moment? I was wondering if you could help me with something."

When she tells me the reason for her call, I'm dumbfounded to say the least. "I'm not sure. She was wearing a dress, true, but I can't tell you if it was expensive or not. I suppose it was evidence, and they gave it back to her later? You should call her."

"Yes, I'll do that." Kelli sighs. "It was a reach. I guess I just wanted to hear your voice."

"Nothing wrong with that. How are you holding up? You left early."

"It's all in the caffeine," she says dryly.

"Any news on your partner?"

"Not in a while, but he and the girlfriend are recovering. On your end?"

"Everything is quiet," I tell her. "I can't wait for you to come home."

"Me too. See you later. I love you."

"Love you too."

I see Mom's pensive look, and I wonder if I could use the time to get more stories of rebellion out of her. It's good to finally connect over something, even though she's going home tomorrow.

Chapter Eighteen

Kelli

I t takes me a few more calls to uncover that Emmett's yacht was docked in a luxury marina not far from the harbor where the boat was rented. Circumstantial, the way it always is with him, but I file it away for later.

Next, Annabel. The call I make goes to voicemail, and I leave her a message. *Hi, this is Kelli Jameson. I hope you and Marc are well. When you get this, could you please call me back? This might sound strange, but I have some questions about the dress you wore when you were found.*

Strange, the fact that she would be wearing a dress to go on a boat like that, out at sea. Not so strange if someone put her there, or she was trying to escape. Come to think of it, I should visit the lifeguard too. Everything I needed, the boss said. The other tourists have long left the inn, but the guard on the scene that day is a local.

I call ahead to make sure she's in the office, then leave. It's a ten-minute drive. One upside of police work in a small town—everything is close together, and I won't waste a ton of gas sitting in traffic. It will all be fine once we get rid of Emmett. I feel like we're a lot closer to achieving that goal.

The lifeguard is a brunette woman in her early twenties.

"I'm surprised," she says. "The police already came to talk to me about this."

"I know. I just have a few follow-up questions."

"Sure, go ahead."

"Isn't it a bit unusual for you to be on the beach at this time of year?" It might not be the worst idea to ease her into this, and I'm curious.

"I'm there full time in the summer, but we still make the rounds in the fall. It's pretty cold, but there are some hard-core swimmers with their dry suits," she explains.

"All right. I wanted to ask you about particular details of that day."

"There's nothing more I can tell you," she says with a shrug. "Her boat washed up on the shore, and some tourists called me for help. Ms. Roman was barely conscious. Someone had already called an ambulance, and I stayed with them. Later it turned out that she could go home and...I think she was staying at your parents' place?"

"That's right." In the report, it says that Annabel was dehydrated and underweight, though there were no obvious signs of abuse. How long was she out there? "Do you often fish people out of the sea like that?"

"Sometimes, but usually they aren't people who've been missing for years. Teenagers who party, people who overestimate their skills, that kind of thing. I was wondering what she was doing out there in this weather. I told that to the other cop."

"Do you remember what she was wearing?"

"Yeah, that's strange. A yellow dress—it wasn't suitable for the weather or a trip on the boat, this kind of boat anyway."

That doesn't come as a surprise either. There's a photo in the police file. The material looked wet and colorless. No DNA other than Annabel's.

"This might sound strange, but did you see a designer label?" Of course, none of the officers who were first on the scene connected her to Emmett, so no one thought to check.

"Maybe. I don't know that I would recognize any."

"Is there anything else you can remember from that day?"

Her gaze is pensive. "I wish I could help you, but...no. It was a scene like out of a movie."

"Thank you."

That phrase sticks with me when I drive back to the station—a scene like out of a movie. I've heard that before in the context of this case.

I need to talk to Annabel. I wonder if she was even able to tell if that dress wasn't hers.

Merin

Reluctantly, Kelli admitted that there was no good reason to keep me from doing the tours, and it's only a few more days until we close for the holidays anyway, with reduced hours for the tourist information.

I drive my mother to the airport early in the morning. We part with a hug, on a much better note than I could have hoped for. As much as I wish she could stay longer, I know we've made important progress.

I'm excited. Speaking of which.

We finally put in an offer, and to our surprise, the realtor gave us the good news quickly. I can't wait, and I'm pretty sure Kelli feels the same. I sent her a reminder via text anyway, knowing how preoccupied she is with work.

Fortunately, this tour kicks off with a breakfast at a bakery that's been in the same family for four generations. Their specialty is a pastry that comes in sweet and savory, and my group, all adults this time, indulges heartily. There's an elderly couple among them, and two women in their mid-fifties maybe, obviously a couple too. It makes me feel like I spent a big part of my life under a dome. I understand Kelli's first reaction a bit better.

When George asked me to marry him, I didn't even have to think about it. I liked him. A lot. Even later, I felt for him, knowing that there was no way he could keep his job and be out...Looking back, my motivations might have been a bit sketchy. I was unaware, thinking I was doing a friend I loved a favor.

And year after year another emotion tried making itself known, and I'd only push it deeper and further away.

Until Kelli.

Until all my delusions came tumbling down, and with them, one of the two only homes I'd ever known.

I force myself back to the present and reality. It's a cold but clear day, perfect for a brisk walk.

"Okay, I think we've all warmed up. Who's ready to explore?"

They all look eager and excited. The woman in the elderly couple told me she used to be a history teacher, like me.

For a while, I actually forget the dire reality of Emmett's crimes, and even the responsibility of choosing and, in the future, paying for, a home. I love talking to the small but receptive group, their hunger for information and stories.

Everyone comes up to the lighthouse to hear me explain the works of it, and the story of Louisa Bennett.

"You can see the inn from here," Wendy, one of the women remarks. "I imagine many of the other houses hadn't been built yet."

"Except for some of the businesses we saw in town, almost none. Louisa became friends with the innkeeper at the time. Mrs. and Mr. Jameson bought it from one of her descendants."

"Friends, under these circumstances, that's...romantic?"

"It could have been," I say, "but we don't know. For sure, they were two of the few women business owners in town, and we can imagine they had to stick together."

She and her partner share a smile that isn't hard to interpret.

"You can find a bit more at the local library. I'm afraid there's nothing 100% conclusive."

"We can work with subtext, right? Since we've been doing that forever."

I smile at them, but I can't help wondering what they'd think of my story.

"Something we know for sure is that Louisa got to enjoy this view for almost thirty years."

"That's all interesting, but haven't you had a modern-day mystery recently? A woman who washed up on the shore?" a man, early forties, asks, jolting us out of our musings about Louisa.

"I'm afraid that's not part of the tour."

"But it happened not far from here?" he presses.

"It's true. You see the inn is over there, and tourists pulled her to safety on the beach below. I think it's time we all go back down now. We have a couple more places to visit."

Aside from the man's question, the morning is blissfully uneventful.

That is, until one of my eager participants doesn't watch their step and slips. As if in slow motion, the man tumbles down a small ravine and with a splash, lands in the creek that leads into a pipe, and then the sea from here. Since the tide is low, so is the water level. Thank God for favors big and small.

"Mr. Hendricks! Are you hurt?"

He's already on his feet.

"No, just wet and embarrassed," he laughs.

"We're almost at the inn. We can get you dry clothes and a cab there."

"Sounds like a plan." Why isn't he coming up? His gaze is drawn to something close to the pipe—or inside? "I don't know," he says, sounding uneasy now. "Someone should come down here and take a look. I don't think this belongs."

I pray it's not a dead body.

"You should come up and walk to the inn with us. The water will come up at some point."

"Then let's call the police real quick. This stuff shouldn't be in here."

My fingers are already on the screen of my phone. At least he said, stuff. Not a person.

Chapter Nineteen

Kelli

M erin and I exchange a wry smile before she instructs the other members of the tourist group to join her at the inn after we're done. She's off with a shivering Mr. Hendricks to make sure he doesn't catch a cold or worse from his unexpected tumble.

Meanwhile, I take a look at the bundle that Manning and I have unearthed, carefully, from inside the pipe. One more high tide, and it might have been gone forever.

We'll take a closer look after we get it to the lab, but we can see there are black clothes inside, a black baseball cap and glasses, and a couple of firearms.

The pipe seems like an interesting hiding place if you're unaware of tides.

I was right. The recent crime spree has nothing to do with anyone local, and everything with Emmett and the goon he paid to go after Marc Roman, and Ryan Heller. Either said goon was careless, or he counted on the sea washing away evidence. If he works for Emmett, he has nearly unlimited resources. I hope that we're lucky again and find more DNA on these items, something to identify the attacker. If the county lab treats this as the emergency it is, we'll have results soon.

⟨◦⟩

Before checking on things at the inn, I swing by the hospital once more. Heller is awake, but groggy. His sister Dolores is with him.

"Hi," she greets me. "I didn't think we'd meet again so soon, under such lousy circumstances."

That about sums it up.

"Your brother's tough. It's a good thing because I need him back at work soon."

"I don't know about that," Heller says. "I hear you got a lead on the shooter?"

"This one was lucky," I tell him. "A tourist tumbling down into a creek and finding clothes and a weapon. We're going to search the area some more, and each item in that bag is being examined right now."

"See," he says to his sister. "She's got it all covered."

"We'll see about that. I know someone asked your girlfriend already. She said you take care of the security system. Is there any chance..."

"That I forgot? No." Heller's denial is swift and convincing. "They disabled or hacked it. When the backup came in, *they* set off the alarm. That asshole didn't."

The set-up of the attack was elaborate. Something like that doesn't come cheap.

"We're a lot closer to catching him now. I'll keep you updated," I promise.

I already suspect that we won't find much more evidence in the field. We'll have to wait.

At the inn, Mr. Hendricks accepts a dry, clean change of clothes that Dad managed to find him.

"You have time for a quick coffee?" Dad asks after Hendricks has left.

I check my phone and decide that the answer is yes. Nothing new on any front. The lab will take a bit longer. Emmett isn't on the move, and Annabel hasn't called me back yet.

"Have you decided on the house?" Mom asks as she pours all of us a cup. A plate with cookies and pastries appears alongside the coffee. I almost forgot about this, but it's true: There will be a life after this case. *Repeat after me.*

"We have," I share the news. "We put in an offer, and it was accepted. The realtor called to meet us tonight."

I see the way Merin's face lights up. This was without a doubt one of the best decisions I, we, have ever made.

"Will you have to do a lot of work?" Dad asks.

"Some, but there's nothing urgent. We can do renovations as needed. So far, nothing's falling down..." I wince. That was the worst possible metaphor.

Merin laughs. "Don't worry, I didn't think you were making fun of my previous house coming down. And the silver lining is," she explains for my parents' benefit, "some of the insurance money can go towards the down payment."

"Great," Dad says. "Something to celebrate once you close. Mom and I will keep the champagne cold."

We are really going to do this, as soon as tonight.

"Did someone say champagne?" Fiona has come to the table.

"Not for you," Merin says. "Your mother is going to have my hide."

It's not an exaggeration, given that Fiona and her friends had the habit of meeting in an old shack in the woods to drink and plot revenge for one of them.

Mom, of course, doesn't know the whole story.

"I'm not for encouraging underage drinking," she says, "but maybe half a glass won't hurt. Not more, young lady."

"Yes, Ma'am."

I have to leave the cozy scene and go back to the job. But eventually, I'll come back to Merin, and our home, every day. It's something to aspire to.

Going back to the station, I take the long route past the house Emmett has rented.

I won't be much longer, I promise. Him. And myself.

<hr>

The results from the county lab hadn't come in when I left that evening. I spent a couple of hours out near where the man's clothes and weapon were found, to no avail. Emmett didn't leave the house once.

Coming back to the cute, charming house already feels different. We'll be able to use a lot of my furniture, which is just as well given the investment we're going to make. Eventually, we'll add different pieces, maybe from some local businesses.

"This is really where we're going to live."

Merin sounds happy, almost reverent. I plan to revere her tonight. The thought puts a smile on my face.

"You are doing the right thing," the realtor assures us. "Even if you change your mind a few years down the line, you could always rent it out. The demand isn't going away, and perhaps I shouldn't say this because you'd be your parents' competition—those who rent out here are pretty much always booked."

"Yeah, but we're not there yet. We really want to live here, make it our own."

Before, I never even thought about buying, let alone in a place this small, and this close to my parents' home and business. Now, it all feels right.

"All right. Congratulations. You got yourself a new home."

Who would have thought that the worst case of my life would lead to this?

⟨⟨⟨⟩⟩⟩

It's not time for celebration just yet. Merin drives on the way home which leaves me some time to indulge further in my plans, until my cell phone rings. It's an unknown number. When I answer, the caller's stark emotion comes through right away, without a doubt. Annabel Roman is terrified and close to tears.

"I'm so sorry I didn't call you back earlier, but I didn't know what to say. It's all horrible."

"Are you okay? Is Marc?"

"Yes. No. He's doing better, but I'm not okay. The nightmares are worse than ever, and I'm not even sure if they are dreams or memories. The water...it's always the water. I'm scared of drowning."

"Annabel, please, slow down. Are you safe right now?"

"I guess. I'm at home. Everything is locked."

"Okay. You got my message?"

"About the dress? I tried so hard to think about it, but then I got scared. It doesn't even make sense. I'm losing my mind."

"I don't think that's the case," I try to calm her. "I think your mind is trying to make sense of what happened to you, and it's giving you clues. Are you seeing someone about it?"

"Of course." I can't blame her for her resignation. I can't even imagine being in her situation. "You wanted to know about the dress. They gave it back to me, and I tossed it in the back of my closet. I don't even remember buying it, not that it means anything. I could have just forgotten like everything else."

I'm reminded of when I visited Erica McQuade's home. I hated having to ask her questions that would draw her back into the traumatic experience. I had to, in order to put the pieces together. Then. Now.

"Could you do me a favor, and check the label? See if anything rings a bell?"

Annabel laughs bitterly. "I've been waiting so long for that magic bell to ring. It's probably futile but give me a minute."

After about three minutes, she's back and reads me the label of the dress. "That's expensive, right? I know that Dan would expect me to wear stuff like that, but I could never afford it."

"You remember him a little, don't you? You think he bought it for you?"

"He might have. I'm not sure. I do remember something. Him, talking about that cop always being on his case. Or did I make that up?"

"Give yourself time to sort it all out," I advise. Meanwhile, I plan to make sure that Emmett will never be a threat to her again. The sinking feeling in the pit of my stomach tells me that he's no longer interested in Annabel. He's still here, still planning on terrorizing the town—and me, that cop, always on his case. "Thank you so much for talking to me. I wish you all the best."

Did she mix that up? As far as I know, Emmett was investigated for the first time after Annabel went missing. What cop was he talking about, if not me, but more importantly, when did he say those words to her? When he was already holding her someplace? Before?

We have arrived at the inn by the time I find the designer label online. Those dresses are in the four to five figures. This has

Emmett's signature written all over it, though it will be hard to trace one particular item back to him. There are far more ridiculously wealthy people buying this stuff.

Merin sneaks a glance. "I'd like to remind you that we just bought a house. I don't think we could afford those...ever."

"Could you see me in one of those? It's the brand Emmett bought for Annabel. If I'm not mistaken, this was part of Chloe Banks' wardrobe too."

"He's a control freak," Merin surmises. "He wants the women to feel like they owe him."

"He believes everyone in the world owes him," I say. "But you're right. There's something there."

"And you're going to find it. Now, let's celebrate that we have a new home?"

"Of course." I give her a smile, willing to push all other questions aside for the moment. Home, it means a lot to both of us, but even more so to Merin who lost hers.

We'll have a lot of work to do, but this is a moment to cherish.

⁂

"This is a really great Christmas present," Mom says when I'm talking to her later. "You found a home here, and someone to share it with. So, the wedding is next summer?"

I nearly choke on the champagne. "Wow, slow down. We haven't talked about this yet."

"Well, you should," she says bluntly. "You know that while people are laid back here, it's always best to protect what you have."

"I'm not sure how Merin feels about it."

"How do you feel about it?"

"I'd do it in a heartbeat," I confess. "Before the new year even. But I have to go at her pace, and we'll both have to figure out what marriage even means to us."

"Sure," Mom acknowledges. "Don't make it too complicated though. It's always about a partnership, and I don't think Merin looks back with a lot of regrets. It was just different."

"Different? They were both scared. They had to hide from the world, worse, their own families. I'm glad Merin and her mother made up, but..." I leave the meaning hanging in the air, but Mom caught it.

"That's for her to forgive, not you," she reminds me calmly.

"I guess you're right. If it makes you feel any better, I'll talk to her about that summer wedding."

She laughs. "You better work on your proposal."

I will. First, I need to catch a kidnapper and murderer.

Chapter Twenty

Once the DNA results come in, we finally get a break. The investigator from the county got a hit, and he has brought in a man with a considerable rap sheet. I'm going to meet him at his precinct but make a quick stop at the hospital first.

Heller groans when I tell him the news.

"Really? The first and probably only big case we ever get here, and I have to sit it out because some asshole shot me."

"I'd find different words," his girlfriend says dryly. "Thanks for everything, Detective Jameson. You really think they caught the right guy?"

"DNA doesn't lie." It's an old line, but it still holds merit. The man in custody is the one who hid those clothes in the pipe, likely wore those clothes while committing several crimes. I'm optimistic. "This will be over soon. I hope you can enjoy the holidays, despite everything."

She sighs. "We plan to. After we survived this, I'll shut up everyone who complains about calories this Christmas."

"As you should. I'll talk to you later."

Detective Jasinski, the investigator from the county was supposed to come to town—now it's a good thing that he didn't. He offers me coffee in the break room while we update each other on the latest findings.

It's time to have another go at Mr. Alan Raynor. So far, he hasn't talked. He hasn't asked for a lawyer either. I assume when you work for Emmett, the risk is always on your side. He can't hope that Emmett might send one of his own, high-priced attorneys. I hope that will work in our favor.

Then Jasinski and I return to the interrogation room, and it's my turn with the suspect.

"Good morning, Mr. Raynor."

Other than him checking me out, there's no notable reaction from him when I walk into the room.

"Detective Jasinski tells me you're not interested in a conversation. I assume that means you're ready to go down for whoever hired you. Perhaps you even have a nice sum of money stashed away somewhere, though it might take a long time to get near that. If you ever make it."

"What kind of bullshit is that?" he asks. He doesn't fool me. I can detect the anger simmering just beneath the calm, nonchalant façade.

"Bullshit? We got your DNA on the weapon used in an attempted murder. A local cop and his girlfriend? That won't go over so well with the judge. We have the knife you used to attack Marc Roman too." No DNA on that one, but he has to know the evidence against him is piling up—and there won't be anyone bailing him out.

"I don't know who these people are," Raynor scoffs. "You're wasting your time."

"To be honest, I don't think so. But I have good news for you."

"So, you're letting me go?"

"Tell us who hired you. We're interested in the big fish, and you can deliver them. That's the only thing you can do for yourself."

"Bite me. I want the public defender now. You don't know shit."

I take a look at Jasinski, and he nods.

"You can call them now," he says. "Could take a while though. Why don't you tell us what we know nothing about?"

"Why don't I shut up altogether?" Raynor fires back. "You're trying to trip me. I didn't do anything."

"The evidence says otherwise," I say. "You really want to spend decades in prison because of one job? Emmett has done this multiple times. You're expendable to him."

He stares back at me with a sullen expression, but I didn't miss the minute reaction, the widening of his eyes at hearing the name.

"I don't know who that is. You want to threaten me, lady? It's not working. The PD will have me out of here in no time."

I'm afraid that it's not entirely unrealistic.

❧

"What's your impression?" I ask Jasinski while Raynor is on the phone with the PD.

"He's lying through his teeth."

"Oh, good. People have told me I might be paranoid."

"I don't think you are," he says. "I'm not sure it was wise to mention Emmett."

"Why?"

"He's not going to give him up. There's too much on the line. If Emmett is as smart as you say he is, he's always covering his tracks. Raynor knows it too, and the last thing he wants is to become a loose end."

"We need to shake something loose. He's safe here for now, isn't he?"

"As long as Emmett doesn't think he'll talk."

I don't say "what if" out loud, but my thoughts must have been obvious. Jasinski shakes his head. "He's a suspect. We still won't use him as bait, and as far as I'm informed, you should be staying away from Emmett." He holds up a hand when I'm about to protest. "Yes, I know your boss signed off on it, but everyone agrees this only works if you're not too visible to Emmett. That's why I thought you shouldn't have mentioned his name this early."

I can see his point, though I consider mine still valid. Raynor might ask his PD to get a message back to Emmett...and that's where we could catch him. There's a wealth of opportunities and future plans lying on the other side of that threshold.

Moving into our new home.

Asking Merin to marry me...but I can't think of this now.

"What's the game plan?"

"You go home, monitor the situation for now. We'll see if Mr. Raynor is more eager to talk once he's more aware of his options. The public defender will lay it out for him, and if he understands it's looking dire..."

I'm torn. I want to be here and stay up to date, but Emmett is still around. I don't know why, and it's bothering me. Yes, it's better to be home.

I drive straight to the station where I stand in front of the board I created. Five years ago, Annabel went missing. Last year, Chloe Banks. Found dead six weeks later in an abandoned warehouse, wearing designer gear and make-up. The shoes are from the same label as Annabel's yellow dress.

Marc Roman, attacked in broad daylight. Dan Heller and his girlfriend Liz, shot by an intruder who managed to disable the security system, but enabled it again on his way out.

Over at the county, they are looking at Raynor's finances right now. Unlike the designer wear Emmett bought the women, those black clothes are fairly common. Even the gun is something you can get legally, for cheap, considering.

We need to find the link between Emmett and Raynor.

I know it's there.

I call Annabel again and catch her sounding tired and dispirited.

"It's you again. I'm sorry, I have nothing to help you."

"Could I just send you a picture, and you tell me if he's familiar?"

"I guess I can't stop you. Go ahead."

"Thank you. This will help."

After I send the image, a few seconds tick by before I realize she's ended the call. When I try again, I get the message that the number is not available at the moment. Annabel turned off her phone.

I can't ignore what just happened, so I call Roger.

"Hey," I say without greeting. "I need someone to check on Annabel Roman. It's important. She just hung up on me."

"And I'm tempted to do the same. We can never get rid of you, can we? Just kidding, Kelli. I know you're still working the case. Is she in danger?"

"I don't think so, but I sent her the picture of a suspect. We think that he attacked Marc Roman, a local cop, and his girlfriend on Emmett's behalf."

"So much for slow pace," he comments.

"Can't help it if the case followed me here. You're going to check on her?"

"Yes, of course. I'll get back to you."

That being taken care of, I can finally go home. Just when I've parked the car, the phone rings again.

"I win," the high-pitched voice says, sounding more than a cartoon character than a person.

I get out of the car as fast as humanly possible and jog all the way up the stairs and into the inn.

Mom gives me a quizzical look from where she's putting more decoration on the reception desk.

"Everything okay?"

"That's my line. Are Merin and Fiona upstairs?"

"Helping Dad to prepare dinner. Everyone's fine. Why?"

"No reason."

I call it in anyway and give the number, though I don't have much hope. It will be a burner phone.

What is he trying to do other than mess with my mind?

❦

We're fine. Everyone is fine. Just Emmett trying to taunt me. By the time we have had dinner and retreated to Merin's room, I managed to calm down.

"I can't believe that starting next month, we can get started, clean up, move in some things." Merin's tone is dreamy. I get dreamy. For the past hour or so, I finally managed to push the creepy warning out of my mind.

"Why not start tomorrow?"

"Because it's Christmas Eve. I think your parents would like us to be here."

"Right."

"You didn't forget?"

I kiss her tempting lips. "You make me forget everything."

"I don't know if that's a good thing or not," she says, self-conscious. "You didn't hear anything from your old colleague?"

"No, but I trust him. He'd tell me if there was anything new."
As if on cue, the phone starts to vibrate on the nightstand. For a few seconds, I stare at it with resentment.

"It's all right, get it," Merin advises, pulling the sheet up around her. "The sooner this is over, the better."

Truer words...It's Roger, telling me that Annabel is safe and sound at home, and she apologizes for hanging up on me.

She says he reminded her of a face in her nightmares, and that it had to do with water. Very vague. Couldn't identify him as the man who attacked her brother though.

I ponder this. Given the fact that the attacker—Raynor, most likely—wore a cap and glasses, I didn't think she would identify him from the photo. If he's been around Emmett, doing his dirty work for a while, it would make sense that his picture triggers a reaction—fear.

But those memories come back to her in bits and pieces, and no one can say how long it will take until we have a more complete picture. If Emmett was done here, he wouldn't still be living in the rented house.

No, he's up to something. At least Merin will be off work for a few days. The weather is going to take a turn for the worse over the holidays. We have to hope for another breakthrough.

"I know you want it to go faster," Merin says, reading my mind. "But you've made a lot of progress since Annabel first arrived."

"Too many people have gotten hurt." I don't mean to argue. I'm just tired.

"We're still going to celebrate Christmas. Emmett will have to lay low now that you caught Raynor."

"Let's hope so."

I win. I still fear that he considers me his direct opponent, and he will use whatever he can to make me lose his game. I take in

Merin next to me. My future is with her. I can't afford any more mistakes.

Chapter Twenty-One

Merin

Kelli needs distraction, and I'm more than willing to do whatever I can to make that happen. It's my pleasure. Of course.

We fall back asleep, and a good twenty minutes later, when I'm about to get up, Kelli tugs on my hand, and I tumble back into bed with her, giggling.

"We can't. If we don't hurry up, we'll be late to the breakfast table, and everyone will have an idea why."

"That bothers you?" she asks with an inviting smile.

I'm easily tempted, but I'm also easily flustered, and this is an important day.

"Maybe a little," I admit. "I don't know. In any case, I'm hungry, and we have to get ready first."

"Yeah," she agrees with a sigh.

I'm still giddy as I head to the bathroom.

I can't wait for the first Christmas morning with her. During the past few days, I spent a bit of time during my breaks shopping for gifts, Fiona, something for my mom that Fiona will give her once she's back, another for both my parents. Ellen and Drew. Kelli's parents. A little something for Sally I'll give her once I'm back at work. I sent George a gift certificate with his greeting card, something without the complicated emotional entanglement that connected us once.

And Kelli, of course.

I can't wait.

Kelli's parents offer an early dinner for the guests that stay over the holidays, then, later, we'll have dinner as a family. I like the sound of that. There's a lot to prepare and cook, and I'm more than happy to help, knowing my efforts will be appreciated.

The two women who were fascinated by Louisa's story and the possible romance with the innkeeper, are still here as well. I wonder if their family's views on their relationship have something to do with it. If that's the case, I hope they have the best Christmas ever in this raw, beautiful environment, in a place where it's beyond a doubt that they are welcome. A place rich with myths about a woman loving another woman.

"You know, you don't have to do this," Maxine reminds me as I'm peeling potatoes in the kitchen. It's warm and cozy, smelling delicious already. It reminds me of home. It *is* home.

"No, it's perfect. I love that you give the guests a Christmas dinner. And Kelli still had a few errands to run."

"Did she? I hope she thought about your gift before now."

Her tone makes me wonder if she knows something I don't, and all of a sudden, I hope my surprise will live up to whatever Kelli has planned.

"I'm sure it's not about that. She wanted to drive by the station and check on her colleague."

Maxine sobers up immediately. "Yeah. It's a good thing they found the guy who did it."

"It is." I direct my gaze back to my potatoes.

"I'm sorry, I didn't mean to remind you. We never had anything like that happen here. It's usually much more peaceful. Which makes us even happier that you've chosen to stay."

"Nowhere is one hundred percent perfect. But if I can live and work here, and be with Kelli, it pretty much is." I blush as I become aware of my words. Nevertheless, they're true.

"I think you'll love Kelli's surprise. And no, I'm not going to tell you what it is."

I didn't think she would, but I'm intrigued.

A few minutes later, I have to leave the potatoes behind after all. Eddie Burton calls me from the lighthouse to tell me he has come across some papers that I might find interesting.

"We'd have to verify their accuracy, but if they are for real, they could be a real gem for the museum and your tour. Seems like Ms. Bennett had a hiding place that no one ever found before. They appear to be love letters."

"Really?" I calm my voice after almost squealing with excitement. "What are the odds that you find them on Christmas Eve?"

He laughs at that. "Right? You're probably busy, but I thought you might want to see them right away."

"You're correct about that. Could I keep them over the holidays? I could research places where to have them authenticated, and I swear I'll treat them with the utmost respect."

"I'm sure you will. Yes, come by and get them. I'll be waiting for you."

"Thank you so much. I can't wait."

It occurs to me that in recent years, Christmas was never filled with this much excitement. George and I gave each other gifts because it was expected. We kept them as practical as we could without raising anyone's suspicion.

Books, something for the house, sports gear. All of it gone within minutes, buried under rubble. I force the image out of my mind, but much of my excitement has vanished. I'm not broke or hungry, or homeless. I'm doing much better than I could have expected only a few months ago—and I might be solving a mystery of my own, the relationship between Louisa Bennett and the innkeeper, Marie Germaine.

That doesn't make me a detective, but it's pretty amazing nonetheless.

⁂

There's a doorbell for the museum. I ring it and wait. When there's no answer after a minute or so, I knock.

"Mr. Burton, I'm here!"

I'm about to use my key when I realize that the door isn't locked. This isn't unusual. He does it when he expects me to show up with tourists eager to learn about local history. He probably unlocked it when I assured him that I'd drop what I was doing to come check on Louisa's hidden papers.

It step inside the building. It's eerily quiet.

"Mr. Burton?" I call out. The space is not that big. Unless he went all the way up—but why would he? I take a couple of stairs up, then change my mind. He must be in the museum. Maybe he's on the phone.

I knock on the door that connects the lighthouse with the small addition that houses the museum. It's open, so I go inside.

"Mr. Burton, hi, it's Merin. You have those papers down here?"

I stop cold when I see him stretched out on the floor near the corner with the paintings I regularly show to the groups. I get to my knees beside him, feel for a pulse. I say a prayer when I find it. "Mr. Burton, can you hear me?"

He groans. "Why do you have to yell?"

"What happened? Do you need me to call the police?"

"The police?" His eyes snap open. "Why? I slipped and fell. Damn stupid accident on Christmas Eve."

"You shouldn't..."

He sits up anyway.

"I'm really sorry," I say, my heart still hammering. What was I thinking, that someone attacked him? It would fit right in with the recent events. An accident, I tell myself. Calm down. "I should get you to the hospital, get you checked out."

"I don't need to go to the hospital," he says with a dismissive gesture. "Do you want those papers or not?"

"I definitely want them. But then we go to the hospital. You might have a concussion."

"Pushy woman," he mutters, and despite my initial fears, I have to smile.

"That's my middle name. Come on. The sooner we get you there, the sooner you can go home."

"All right. Let's get those papers first."

The metal box sitting on the table he's pointing to looks antique. I only take a quick look but am already intrigued by the content. I think of the guests at the inn, the couple. Perhaps I can make their Christmas even more interesting.

First things first. I help Mr. Burton into his jacket, and we close up before we leave. It's raining, snowflakes mixed in with the downpour. He's pale. I hope he'll be okay—and that he doesn't throw up in the car. It's still the rental from when I first came here.

"Well, Merry Christmas, Merin." He grins wryly.

"It will be, I promise." We're off to the hospital. It's a good thing there's almost no traffic because I can't see much ahead.

I hope I'll be able to get home soon. There's a lot of work still to do before we can sit down and enjoy.

Briefly, I wonder if Mom and Dad are thinking of me as they, too, prepare food for a house full of guests.

Chapter Twenty-Two

Kelli

When I come back to the inn, the bad weather has arrived. For the next few days, it will be rain, snow, sleet, all mixed together.

The house smells amazing though, like all the Christmases I remember as a child. I assume that the dinner for the guests will start soon. I can hear their excited voices from the breakfast room, feeling all warm and giddy inside. Grateful. Mom and Dad know how to make everyone feel welcome, family, guests, and strangers.

It says a lot about Emmett that they identified him right away as someone they didn't want in their home or business.

I find Mom in the kitchen, standing over giant pots and pans.

"Merin isn't here?" I ask, surprised. "She said she was going to help."

"Yes, and unlike you, she did," Mom says. "Just kidding. She got a call from Eddie at the lighthouse. Something about papers from the lighthouse keeper he found. She went to get them."

I can see how she'd do that, even on this day. Merin has been fascinated with this story, and I understand why. Louisa Bennett's story is as much local history as it is the history of our community. If there's ever proof.

I check the clock. "When was that?"

Mom's gaze follows mine. "About two hours ago? If I remember correctly, she wanted to bring the papers here, to check them out. You better call her? The weather will only get worse."

I'm already clicking Merin's number as she speaks. Two hours is a long time to just get some papers at the lighthouse. If I'm paranoid, so be it. Merin doesn't pick up.

"Do you have a number for Burton?"

"Not that I'm aware of, sorry. Perhaps they found something so intriguing, she forgot the time?"

We both know that's not Merin. She's reliable above all else.

"I'm going to check on her," I say.

"I think that's a good idea. Wait. She has an extra key for the lighthouse. She keeps one with her, but..."

I take the key my mother is handing me, trying to stay rational. I just want to make sure everything's okay. I have big plans for later today.

Merin

I stop and stare for a few seconds, having a hard time believing my eyes. The ER is a lot busier than I expected it to be on this day, at this hour. Someone sneezes, and I take a step back instinctively.

"See?" Eddie sounds almost satisfied. "Are you sure you don't want to be somewhere else? I know I do."

"Funny," I mumble. "Let's get things started." At the nurse's desk, I explain the situation.

"I found Mr. Burton unresponsive at first. He came to quickly, but I'm afraid he might have a concussion."

"This lady here is giving me a bigger headache than my fall," the ungrateful fool says. "Okay, I do have a bit of a headache. I'm fine otherwise. Didn't throw up."

She asks him a few more questions, and convinced that he is in good hands, I tune out for a moment. The story still rings strange to me. He's not exactly frail. How did he fall? Slip? There's nothing to stumble over in the museum. It's a neat place.

I'm brought out of my musings by Eddie loudly complaining again.

"It's Christmas Eve, and you expect me to sit here all day?"

"Sir, a doctor will see you in a bit. It's better that way."

"I'm not going to stay overnight."

I'm about to get irritated. "Eddie. Let them help you, would you? I'll wait with you."

So I do.

Thinking I should probably notify someone about my whereabouts, I get my cell phone out of my purse, realizing I have a few missed messages from Kelli.

It's not quiet in the waiting room, but even so I can sense the urgency. I cast another look at the clock on my phone, suppressing a sigh. I'd feel bad leaving Eddie all by himself, but I feel equally worse having left Maxine with all that work. I have to make it home for dinner at least. I send a quick text to Kelli.

I'm fine, had to take care of something for Mr. Burton. Be home ASAP. I'm sure Maxine told her about the letters, and we can talk about everything else later.

Finally, a doctor is ready to see Eddie. This time I don't hold back the sigh.

It's an interesting Christmas Eve so far.

I, and most of the other occupants of the room, flinch at the harsh bolt of lightning, and the sound of thunder nearby. Only now I realize that the sky outside is a graphite-tone grey.

"Miss? Are you okay?" a concerned voice asks next to me.

For a split-second, I was back home, in that tornado shelter...

"It happens sometimes in the winter," the young woman explains to me nervously. "You're not from around here?"

I manage a smile. "You're right, I'm not, but I just bought a house in town. I guess I'll have to get used to it."

It's not a storm like that. No one's house is going to fall this time.

Kelli

When I arrive at the lighthouse, Merin's car isn't there. She hasn't answered any of my messages yet. I don't want to fear for the worst, but it's hard. There was no sign of a car broken down or an accident on the way.

Merin said that even Emmett might take a break over the coming days, but evil doesn't respect anyone's holidays. In fact, it would make perfect sense for him to strike when people are starting to let their guard down.

Damn it. I call her again, get the voicemail. *Please, call me. I need to know where you are.*

This is when I see the flash of green up on the balcony. It's Merin's coat, but what would she do up there, in this weather? Both she and Burton understand the logistics of this place. What could be so important...or were they surprised by the storm?

I use the key and step inside, take the narrow stairs up. The inside part is no problem. The museum is an addition on the ground level. The next floor, inside the lighthouse, houses the old quarters of the innkeeper. More winding stairs lead to the upper level and outside to the gallery. The door is closed. I can hear the wind howling. It will be worse outside. What happened?

"So sad. Another lost sheep you can't save, Detective Jameson."

At the sound of the voice, I look up, holding on to the railing as Emmett shines a flashlight in my face.

"Where's Merin?"

Standing at the top of the staircase, he has the gall to laugh in my face.

"I'm serious. My colleagues are on the way. You won't get out of it this time."

"Oh, but I think I will," Emmett's tone oozes satisfaction. He's pointing a gun at me.

Carefully, I let my hand fall to my side, and then jump when he pulls the trigger. The gunshot is obscenely loud in the confined space. He hasn't hit me, but it was close. As close as he wanted it to be.

"Don't be ridiculous, Kelli," he yells. "There's a woman out there who doesn't have time for your antics. Now do as I say, or it won't end well for either of you. Keep your hands where I can see them and come up here." I have to be careful. Merin's life—and mine—depend on it.

I was always right about him, but that's cold comfort. He wants the movie ending, the ultimate showdown. If I get it wrong, the villain might win. It's not an option.

"I know she's out there," I say, climbing the narrow stairs slowly. My ears are still ringing. "I saw her coat. The thing about the letters was a hoax, right? Did you kill Eddie?"

"I didn't kill anyone," he claims. "Yet. And the poor sheep isn't Merin, but an unfortunate lady who's a guest of your parents'. It's not personal. I just needed bait, and it worked. Now, let's go enjoy the view with her."

Going out on that platform, with a madman, would be the worst outcome. I can't help that pang of relief when I realize it's not Merin he brought here. For the moment, I don't need a better explanation. We need to get the woman out of the cold, before the exposure gets to her. I don't know how long she's been out there.

"How about we bring her inside, and talk? I assume you want to let me know what the point of all of this is?"

"You'll get the point." He has to almost shout over the wind. "You're going to join her now."

I hesitate, and he yells, "Go, or I'll shoot you right away."

I file away the change of premise. Dan Emmett usually pays people to do the dirty work. He was waiting for me here, with a gun, and a woman he uses as bait. This is personal.

For the moment, I have no choice but to go along. He moves to the side a fraction so I can pass him by.

When I take the first step out on the gallery, I can barely see anything, the icy rain hitting my face creating a painful sensation. I wipe strands of hair back from my face, and for the first time see the woman in the green coat. Not Merin's, though the garment looks similar. I recognize her, Wendy, one of the guests at the inn, who's here over the holidays with her partner.

I look back over my shoulder at Emmett's satisfied grin. I'm too exposed, but what choice do I have?

"What now? What's the plan?" I lower my hands a fraction, and he pushes me hard enough I have to reach for the railing.

"The plan is to make sure you don't do anything stupid, Kelli. Where's the gun?"

"Come on, it's Christmas Eve. I didn't bring one," I try.

"Don't lie to me! Right now, I have a clear shot at both of you. Is that really what you want?"

"Okay."

"Take it out. Slowly. Now throw it in the water."

I curse him and his theatrics, but when I hesitate for a split-second, he fires another shot, so close it's deafening even out here. I can hear Wendy whimper, in pain or fear, I'm not sure. It's a screwed-up dilemma—I need to buy time, but she could already be hypothermic.

I do as I'm told, mentally going over the options I have left.

I have to make him give up his own gun—not very likely—or get to it myself. That's also unlikely, given the narrow space we're in, and the slippery floor underneath our feet. The alternative is to keep him talking until backup arrives. I hope it won't be too late.

The woman watches with wide, frightened eyes. She's shaking hard.

I want to tell her that everything's going to be okay, but she might think I'm mocking her.

"Come on, Emmett," I say, turning to him. "Let's end this right here. We could never get you for Annabel or Chloe. You were angry at me for the investigation, and so you crossed a line. Let her go, and we can work something out."

"You're a liar," he all but spits out the words. "You still don't get it, do you? It has nothing to do with her, or even Annabel anymore. You challenged me to play. You shouldn't have done that if you knew you were a sore loser."

I'm not sure I can follow him all the way into his delusion, but I get a glimpse at the abyss...

"You kidnapped two women, murdered one of them. That's hardly a game."

"It is now. You've been a nuisance since you first came to my office. This ends now." With the gun, he points down. "It ends right here and now, Kelli."

Realization finally hits me. Everything he had Raynor do was merely a distraction, even fostering my fear that he might come after my family. His endgame was this, to get me to this place.

I have no choice but to play my part.

Chapter Twenty-Three

Merin

I have another message from Kelli, urgent this time. *I'm at the lighthouse. Where are you?* I realize my text didn't go through.

Eddie is angry at me because the doctor insisted on keeping him overnight for observation, given his age and overall condition. I say a few apologies, secretly relieved, and leave the hospital. It's true that he shouldn't be home alone.

I should be home by now, but I'll drive by the lighthouse to make sure everything's okay. Then we can finally start the holidays.

I hate to drive in this weather. At least the wind has let up some, a mix of snow and rain still coming down. The lighthouse looms, looking scary in the dark. I see Kelli's car, and another one...My heart leaps into my throat when I recognize the vehicle. It's Dan Emmett's.

I park behind the two cars, get out and run to the door. Before I unlock it, I call 911.

Kelli

"I 'll do what you say, but please, let her go. You don't need her for this. Let her be inside at least. You know she can't go far."

I can see she's shuddering violently. He has tied her wrists and ankles. It's not that warm inside the lighthouse, because no one's living in this building, but getting out of the freezing rain would improve her chances dramatically.

I turn to Emmett and say, "You wouldn't be doing all of this without at least letting me know *how* you won, right? You want me to know. I'll listen."

If she's out of the way, I have a better chance of going for that gun. Once I have it...I can't afford to get ahead of myself. Maybe I'm scared of the alternatives. I'm scared period.

But then, he points to the woman.

"You can get her inside. Hurry up," he yells when I'm slow to react. Her skin is cold and clammy. I have to help her up and all but drag her, because she can't walk with her ankles bound.

"I'm so sorry," I tell her. "We'll get you out of this. I promise." I'm not sure she believes me. But Emmett lets me open the door for her. He's hovering close, still training his gun on me, as she stumbles to the other side.

Standing on the threshold, I think that if it was just me, I would try to make a run for it, but with the hostage, that's not an option.

"Now come back out and close it again!" he shouts.

I can't go back out on that gallery with him again. I know he wants to stage some dramatic fall for me, and if he succeeds, he'll kill her on his way out. I won't let that happen.

Wendy cowers on the floor. I still have one foot inside the room, Emmett sticking so close that I can feel his breath on my neck. I turn around, taking half a step backwards and into the room. Slowly.

"We could sit here for a moment. You could tell me about Annabel and Chloe."

"Are you really that dumb? I thought you got it by now. I showed them a different life. They didn't appreciate it, so I had to show them the alternatives."

"By killing them? How would that help them appreciate what you gave them?"

He doesn't answer, and I'm afraid I'm going to lose him. Maybe there is no answer, other than no one ever held him accountable.

"I couldn't waste all my time on just one of them," he says, as if it's obvious.

"You held them against their will."

He's laughing again, the sound making my stomach churn.

"Against their will? That's a big assumption."

At last, he comes inside as well. As long as we're here, talking, nobody's going to fall to their death.

"It's the yacht, right? You got tired of Annabel and put her on a boat in the middle of the ocean?"

"Wrong. I would have liked her there longer, but she went on that damn boat. Imagine that. Come to think of it, perhaps I should invite you to that yacht, show you everything you still don't understand."

Both of us freeze at the sudden sound and light, the old lighthouse roaring to life. I take advantage of the distraction and lunge at him, the gun cluttering down to the floor through the stairs. My fist connects solidly to his jaw, but then I lose my footing, grabbing the railing with one hand.

I see the fury in his face, realizing that one of us is not going to make it.

Merin

I hope I didn't sound completely hysterical to the 911 dispatcher. It's not hard to interpret the scene unfolding, and we need more officers in here now. In the meantime, all I can do is shine a giant spotlight which I pray will attract attention, and help.

I hear something falling all the way down to the ground floor and use my phone as a flashlight, my heart beating even faster when I realize it's a gun.

I flash back on a scene a few months back, Kelli handing the rifle to me...I'm not helpless. I jog back down the steps, my shoe nearly catching in the metal rungs, but I manage to catch myself. I find the gun and run back up, just in time to see Emmett tumbling backwards. He manages to reach for Kelli's ankle, and they both topple down the narrow stairs.

I rush to her side, distantly noting Emmett lying unmoving on the landing. He has a bleeding cut on his temple. A few seconds, and I can hear him swear. He's not going to be a problem for the moment.

Kelli sits back against the railing, catching her breath. There's a bruise forming on the side of her face, and her expression isn't hiding the pain.

"It's over," is all I can say.

"Yes. It finally is."

"I called 911. They'll be here in a few minutes."

"There's someone up there, a guest from the inn. She was in one of your groups. Could you please check on her?" The tears in her voice might be from the pain. We're all reaching the end of the line, but I have to keep repeating. It's over. I put the gun in her hands and rush up to find one of the women I've been speculating about so much.

Her wrists and ankles have been tied with rope. Fortunately, I know where Eddie keeps a toolkit up here, and I manage to free her from the restraints. Finally, I shut the door to the gallery. There's no doubt she needs to go to a hospital, and soon.

"Help will be here soon. You'll be fine," I promise her.

We both jump when we hear the noise, and I rush to the railing to look down, almost staggering in relief.

The cavalry has arrived, uniformed and plain clothes cops, and paramedics, making their way up.

"Up here!" I shout.

I want to go back to Kelli, but the space is so limited I can't leave my spot until the paramedics get to Emmett's other victim and take care of her.

Even injured, Emmett is loudly protesting his arrest and vows to sue the whole department, the county, the town...I tune him out as I watch a paramedic tend to Kelli. She's shaking her head.

"You're as stubborn as Eddie," I mutter to myself, but despite being cold and running on adrenaline and fear, I have to smile.

Then I can finally go down and find Kelli at the back of the ambulance.

"I'm with her," I announce, warmed at the flash of pride in her expression. It mirrors my own emotion, something long neglected but more welcome than ever.

Chapter Twenty-Four

Kelli

I took a tumble all right, but no one broke their neck or was shot today. We were lucky. I have to remind myself whenever the ambulance hits a pothole and I'm reminded that I'll be black and blue all over for some time. By some miracle, I didn't break anything, only sprained my ankle on the way down about half a flight of those stairs.

It's over. I feel bad for Annabel who will have a load of new trauma to deal with once she remembers. I feel bad for making Mom wait with dinner. To my embarrassment, I feel tears running down my face, hot against my cold skin. I can't stop shivering.

Merin grips my hand tighter.

"We might be late for dinner," she says, "but I'm sure your parents still have some of that chocolate rum for us."

I laugh, and then I can't stop crying.

Fortunately, when we arrive at the hospital, a doctor can see us right away. He checks me out and runs a few tests. After that, I'm good to go, but before we leave, we check on Wendy. Her partner is with her.

"I'm so glad you're okay," Merin says when words still fail me. "And you might be sick of the lighthouse, but when you're back at the inn, could you come see me? I found something about Louisa and Marie."

"We'd love to see that," Wendy says.

Her color is much better, but the angry red lines around her wrists speak of her ordeal.

Emmett took her only one mile away from *The Sand Dollar Inn* where she was doing last-minute Christmas shopping. He'd always planned to lure me there, but to his surprise, I was already headed to the lighthouse, looking for Merin.

Merin came after me. I want to chide her for that, but I can't. She has seen too much. Between tests and exams, I've been on the phone with my boss and Roger, confident that the last strand will be unraveled.

"I talked to my mother," I finally tell the two women. "She's sorry that you're both missing the dinner for the guests, so she wanted me to tell you you're welcome to join us for our Christmas dinner tomorrow. It's no obligation, of course, but she'd love to have you."

Wendy exchanges a look with her partner. "I think I'll be discharged soon, but I don't know...We don't want to impose."

"You're not. The more the merrier."

"Thank you," she says, her look haunted. "I didn't think I was going to make it out."

She, too, will have a lot to deal with.

"But you did. We all did. That's a reason to celebrate."

When we finally make it home, the guests' dinner is long over, and my parents have stashed away their own cooked food in fridge and freezer. Neither of them had much of an appetite between calls from the hospital and the police.

My growling stomach must have given me away.

Mom's eyes are bright, but she laughs.

"I'll warm us something up quickly. It's still Christmas Eve."

"Including dessert and chocolate rum?" I ask, hopeful.

"All included. You two just sit."

With the rush of the last few hours gone, I'm not only hungry, but exhausted. I had such a different day, and night, planned for all of us, following my own errand earlier.

I wanted to say the words the moment it was clear that we'd be all right, but then Merin went to check on Wendy—which, of course, was more important. I told her to.

The paramedics arrived, and the next moment I found myself crying in the back of an ambulance. I'm not even sure I'm done crying. The timing just isn't right.

I'm still antsy, but I'll be okay. All my loved ones are safe, and in one room. We have food and alcohol. For the first time in hours, my nerves begin to settle.

*

There's no way even parts of my elaborate fantasy could come true when every movement still hurts, but I'm happy to just cuddle and fall asleep in Merin's arms. On Christmas morning, I steal out of the room while she's still sleeping soundly, following the wonderful scent of coffee to my parents' kitchen. Mom looks up with a wistful smile when I come in. She's making waffles.

"I can't help it. I know food isn't going to make everything you've been through go away, but I have to make it."

"It goes a long way to help with all the things," I assure her. "You have some Irish Cream liquor?"

"Of course. Chocolate chips and fruit, and whipped cream."

"I didn't have the time to ask her yet, but I will. Soon."

"I'm so happy for you..."

"No, Mom, don't cry. I still have a couple of work calls to do."

"It's Christmas," she says, sounding indignant.

"It will only take a few minutes. Then I'll be ready for a decadent breakfast."

A few minutes later, I have Roger on the phone once more.

"You were right," he says, sounding stunned. "You were always right."

"You don't have to be so surprised."

"The FBI got involved, and we got a warrant for the yacht, last night even."

"That's...good news."

I'm not sure I want to hear the rest, but I have to see it through.

"We'll be working with Annabel to put the pieces together. Get this, he had this whole...area on that damn ship, where he kept the ones he thought might 'appreciate' the lifestyle. There are pictures."

"I'm sorry I'm not much help right now." A part of me, though, is relieved I won't have to deal with these details, likely confirming my worst nightmares.

"Thanks to you, the guy is in jail now. I'd say that's extremely helpful. We talk later?"

"Sure. And Merry Christmas."

"Merry Christmas, Kelli. You did it."

I'm not a coward. I've confronted dangerous criminals, more than once. That other thing shouldn't be so hard, should it?

After breakfast, we exchange gifts. My parents gave us gift cards from just about every shop in town where we'll be able to buy items for the house—and for the bakery that sells the famous pastry. I'll have to rethink my exercise regime after the holidays.

Merin got my parents a restaurant outing, Fiona a collection of books, and the smallest package for me: For a moment I wonder if she got ahead of me, but the necklace with the half-moon is perfect and a reminder only for the two of us.

I thought about giving her that gift during the exchange but reconsidered. I want a more private, more special moment for that. I knew she'd love the dress I bought her because she gazed at it longingly whenever we went past the window in town.

More to come.

This time, there's no evading the work in the kitchen. Okay, truth be told I'm mostly sitting and sampling the goods. I still look rather pitiful, but I'm okay to keep an eye on pots, and the oven. Merin is glowing. I wasn't always unselfish about it but asking her to come here was the best thing I could have done, for both of us.

Earlier, Dad went to get Mr. Burton, who was released from the hospital and will join us for dinner, as well as Wendy and her wife. Fiona slept in, but she, too, helps, setting the table in the dining room.

"Mom says hi," she says. "She wants you to send pictures of the new house ASAP." There's a whole lot more between the lines, something that makes Merin lay down the dishtowel and stand in the middle of the room as she absorbs the meaning of Fiona's words. I get up, wince, and embrace her.

Chapter Twenty-Five

Merin

T he day just flies by. Not much longer, and we head upstairs to change for dinner. The guests have arrived, and
before we go back down, I grab my notes.

"When did you have time to do all that?" Kelli asks with
unveiled admiration. She's one to talk.

"Last night while you were sleeping. I couldn't...and I
thought it was fitting."

"So, they were a couple after all," she concludes.

"It sure sounds like that in the love letters. Nothing graphic,
but it's quite beautiful."

"Just like you."

Her expression is serious, and I wonder what's on her mind.
Then she smiles.

"Let's go. I'm hungry."

"When aren't you?" I tease her.

With Wendy at the table, we can't completely shut out the
all the drama and traumatic events. I think of Annabel and her
brother.

There's no doubt though. We persevered. And my sister wants to talk to me again, soon.

I couldn't be happier.

Kelli

I loved listening to Merin talk about Louisa Bennett, her courage to brave the elements for decades—and to love another woman, innkeeper Marie Germaine. The language the two women used for each other leaves little doubt.

The lighthouse continues to be a symbol of perseverance, of love over hate.

I am so in love that the next step seems only logical, but I have to postpone it once more. The doorbell rings. Conversations around the table come to a halt when Dad brings Bill Cheney into the dining room. My jaw drops.

He should be busy right now, not have the time to chide me for anything. He's not my boss anymore.

"Detective Jameson, I was hoping I could talk to you for a minute."

I catch Merin's look, pensive and worried. There's nothing he can do. More importantly, there's nothing Dan Emmett can do to him or his career.

"Let's go into the kitchen," I suggest. This is beyond strange, standing at the counter with my old boss, here at my parents', on Christmas Day.

"How can I help you?"

"I misjudged you," he says. "I wanted to apologize in person."

I'm not sure I want or need to have this conversation. Too little too late. On the other hand, it's Christmas, so I might just as well hear him out.

"Thank you. I understand that you had a lot of things to consider." Politics. Optics. "For some time, we didn't have all that much to go on."

"But you wouldn't give up. That woman sitting at your dining table is alive because of it, and God knows how many others."

"We can't know. I didn't have the impression he'd stop."

"No, he wouldn't have," he agrees.

"You saw the yacht?"

"I did. Anyway, we'll expect the reports from your side as soon as possible."

"Of course."

"Thanks, Detective. Until then, enjoy the holidays."

"Wouldn't you like to eat with us, Lieutenant?" Dad asks. "We have more than enough."

Everyone is welcome here, but I'm still a little relieved when he declines. To me, he says, "I always believed that grieving parents deserved closure. You gave that to the Gavins and the McQuades, and everyone involved was held accountable. Don't ever doubt that."

"I'm glad to hear that, Sir," I say. Until now, I didn't realize how much I needed to hear it.

I see him out and return to my family.

"We can probably rent a truck to get the rest of your furniture," Merin muses as she looks at the various gift cards. Still wearing my Christmas gift, she's looking beyond beautiful. I could look at her all night…and I might have overdone it a bit, because she gives me a questioning look. "You don't think so?"

"Oh no," I hurry to say. "I just imagine you driving a truck, and I realize that makes total sense."

"People might have been a bit close-minded, but they know how to drive and to shoot," she says.

"To some extent, that's people everywhere." We're getting off topic. "I'll have to write some reports, but I think I can make time next week, so we get all that stuff. Most of it is fairly neutral, so it won't clash with anything that's already in the house."

"I'm sure it will be fine. I can't wait."

"Merin."

"Are you all right? Are you in pain?"

"No. I've had enough painkillers and wine to take care of that. But there is something I meant to ask you." I clear my throat. "I meant to get down on one knee for that, but I hope you won't mind if I don't. That might be painful."

"Oh my God, Kelli."

Her hand goes to her mouth, and for a terrifying moment, I'm not sure if she's excited or scared.

"I know that this subject has a lot of different connotations for you. You probably have mixed emotions about it, but like the house, I believe that we can make it our own, define it the way we see fit. Merin—"

"I say yes," she interrupts me.

"You do?"

"What do you think? Of course. I want to live in that house with you and be married. I love you. That's all the definition I need." She stops herself, looking self-conscious all of a sudden. "I didn't ruin your proposal, did I?" she asks worriedly.

"No, you didn't." I get up and pull her close for a kiss while I take the small box out of my pocket. "But it's not over yet."

Her eyes light up at the sight of the ring. It's a heady feeling to put it on her finger. I've never been so sure of anything in my life.

"You know," Merin says, "I've been thinking about marriage a lot. For some time, I just thought that the real deal wasn't for me, but I realized I was wrong. That's when...I bought you a ring, but I was too chicken to give it to you this morning. Or at any moment before now."

It comes in a small velvet bag, the design matching the necklace that she did give me.

"This moment is perfect," I say.

Outside, the rain has turned into snow, casting the scenery in a soft light.

I lean in until our lips touch, softly at first, and then I kiss her the way I've wanted to all evening. We can hear bits of laughter and Christmas music from downstairs, but all I care about is Merin here in my arms.

For two people who didn't think they deserved a happy ending, we're doing pretty well.

Acknowledgments

T hank you –

As always, Dominique, for everything (including the beautiful cover art!).

To the sapphic fiction community for giving my stories a home.

I couldn't do this without your support.

About the Author

B arbara Winkes writes sapphic crime drama and Christmas romance. She loves writing characters who get the job done, whether it's stopping a predator or saving cherished traditions—while still making time for love. She lives with her wife in Quebec City.

barbarawinkes.com

Also by Barbara Winkes

Kelli & Merin
Thunder

The Crossing Lines Trilogy
Undercover
Redemption
Vengeance

The Connected Series
Promised to the Queen
Drawn to the Enemy
Tempted by the Protector